THE VIDEO WATCHER

THE VIDEO WATCHER

SHAWN CURTIS STIBBARDS

A JOHN METCALF BOOK

BIBLIOASIS
WINDSOR, ONTARIO

FIRST EDITION

Library and Archives Canada Cataloguing in Publication

Stibbards, Shawn Curtis, 1975-, author
    The video watcher / Shawn Curtis Stibbards.

Issued in print and electronic formats.
ISBN 978-1-77196-019-9 (pbk.).--ISBN 978-1-77196-020-5 (ebook)

    I. Title.

PS8637.T515V53 2015   C813'.6   C2014-907959-1
                                              C2014-907960-5

Edited by John Metcalf
Copy-edited by Jesse Eckerlin
Typeset by Chris Andrechek
Cover designed by Kate Hargreaves

Biblioasis acknowledges the ongoing financial support of the Government of Canada through the Canada Council for the Arts, Canadian Heritage, the Canada Book Fund, and the Government of Ontario through the Ontario Arts Council.

PRINTED AND BOUND IN CANADA

To My Grandmother

During the years when I found it necessary to revise the circuitry of my mind I discovered that I was no longer interested in whether the woman on the ledge outside the window on the sixth floor jumped or did not jump, or in why. I was interested only in the picture of her in my mind: her hair incandescent in the floodlights, her bare toes curled inward on the stone ledge.

—Joan Didon,
The White Album

1

Nobody talks to each other at UBC. There are frat-house parties and Wednesday Nights at The Pit and faculty beer gardens, but nobody really talks. I remember I took Damien out there once to watch my car while I bought books, and he said that everyone looked so alone—and it was true.

But when I got back to North Van that spring, it wasn't any better there.

Don't think, I told myself as I locked the front door and started down the driveway, swinging the bag with the Guinness four-pack and humming a riff from Sabbath's "War Pigs."

On Capilano Road a red Beemer shot by me, then a Jetta. I took a deep breath and tried to empty my mind.

Cam will be back in three weeks. It will be different then.

A high-school girl with dusty blond hair was walking on the other side, going in the opposite direction. She walked quickly, her shoulders drawn back, and the gray Champion sweatshirt she wore was loose, and her breasts, round and full, bounced as she broke into a jog.

I was staring at her breasts when I realized that I wasn't thinking of anything else. That thought made the other thoughts come back.

But they were not as strong as before, and I knew there would be too much going on at Alex's to think too much. Green strips of dusk sky glowed between the hemlocks. I thought of myself as some character out of a movie, some angst-ridden character moving from scene to scene. It was always easier when I thought of myself as someone else.

Almost all the high school kids were outside smoking a joint someone had brought. That was Alex's mother's one rule: pot had to be smoked outside. Alex had joined them, and while she was out there I stayed in the kitchen with Diane (which is what her mother insisted we call her). She was making a pitcher of Tang. "So... you moved back to your aunt's house?" she asked.

My eyes fell to the small bulge of flesh between her tight T-shirt and jeans. "Actually, it was my parents'," I said. "We've been renting if for awhile. Now we're just... um... staying there long enough so that my aunt can claim it as her principle residence." I was surprised how effortlessly these words—my aunt's—fell out. "Then sell it. It's some kind of tax thing."

"She knows the angles," Diane said, filling the pitcher with water. "How long she's been in real estate now?"

The sugar swirling in the orange liquid reminded me of a scene in *Citizen Kane*. "I don't know. Since before I can remember, I think."

"Your aunt must be pretty successful. Seems like we always have something around here with her name on it. Or picture. Calendars... pens..."

"Yeah," I said.

One of the girls at the table behind us let out a shrill laugh.

"She says—" I pulled my eyes off them "—if you want to be successful, you got to advertise a lot."

"Do you think this is strong enough?" Diane poured some Tang in a blue Dixie cup and gave it to me. I took a sip. "Mmm. Good," I said.

"I think it's really great that your aunt supports herself like that," Diane continued, her tone making it sound like my aunt was some kind of rock star or celebrity, "Self-reliant. Independent. I keep telling Alex about those things. This—" she nodded to the group of kids huddled around the patio table outside. A boy with a red baseball hat strained to reach something and a tall boy shoved him back "—I hope, is just a phase she's going through."

"I—"

"I thought when Alex got the job at the library," she continued, "she'd meet...a better group of people—though I guess she met you."

Uncertain if this was a compliment or not, I gave a weak smile.

Diane needed to use "the little girl's room," and I got one of the cans of Guinness from the fridge and joined the girls at the table.

The one who was talking the most (the short fat one) sat sideways in her chair, facing the other girl. Her bright red hair was short, and looked dyed, and her round fat face was almost white.

Her eyes fixed on me as I dropped into the chair. "No, I *wouldn't* Kirsten."

The brunette opposite me, the one I found attractive, said, "Whatever."

Silence fell on the table.

I felt myself growing tense.

"What are you talking about?" I asked.

The fat one bit the inside of her bottom lip. "Nothing," she said.

"The apartment," the one called Kirsten said.

The other girl glanced nervously at her and back at me. "It's nothing," she said.

"So why aren't you two outside with the others?"

The short fat girl shrugged and started to chew on her little finger. "Pot sucks. It's juvenile. It's like—for fucking Grade 8s."

"We've got some 'shrooms," Kirsten said coolly. "We're going to do them later."

"'shrooms?" I asked.

"Yeah, 'shrooms,"

She was watching as I opened the Guinness. I pretended not to notice and poured the beer into the glass, studying the head as it formed on the surface.

"What's that?"

"Guinness—you know, stout."

"What?" the fat one said, leaning forward to look.

"Stout, a type of beer."

"It looks like coffee."

I remembered trivia my grandfather had told me about the Guinness family and began to say, "You know the Lions Gate—"

"Did you hear?" the fat one said, pulling both feet up on the chair. As she told Kirsten about a girl they knew, Sabrina, who went down on this guy in his late forties, I was suddenly conscious again of how tedious this party was. I wanted to get up and leave.

But the thought of the empty rooms, the silent hallways, the hours between now and when I might sleep, made me reconsider.

"So," I said, forcing myself to speak, "what were you talking about before? The apartment—"

"It's nothing," the fat one said and shot her friend an anxious glance.

Before I could think of how else to bring up the topic, she asked, "Do you go to Handsworth?"

"I graduated."

"I haven't seen you there."

"I went there last year."

"Did you change schools?"

"I'm at UBC."

"Like, who'd you hang out with?"

I took a large sip of the Guinness. "Cam White... Damien Burgess..."

"Cam White. Isn't he... that psycho?"

"Psycho?" Kirsten looked bemused. "You think everyone's psycho."

"I heard he smashed the window of Tiff's Porsche."

It had been Damien who'd broken the windshield.

"Who—"

"That wasn't him," I said.

"Who was it?"

"I don't know, but it wasn't him."

"I thought he was hot," Kirsten said quietly.

"What! Who? Cameron White?"

Kirsten replied by raising her right hand and wiping a strand of hair from her narrow face, and recrossing her arms.

"You have an accent," the fat one said, leaning over the table and tucking her feet under her. "Like, where are you from?"

"Nowhere. Here."

"No, before here."

"Nowhere."

"So you've lived your whole life here?"

I nodded, anticipating the next three questions.

"Okay, how about your parents? Where are they from? Do they have accents?"

"No. Here."

"So you've lived here your whole life?"

"Yup."

Neither one had a response to this. A notepad advertising my aunt lay on the table and I pulled it over and began to doodle, drawing a moustache on Kris's face and filling in one of her eyes.

"I know someone *else* who has an accent," Kirsten said, threateningly.

"Would you shut up about that."

"So what goes on there," I asked—I assumed they were talking about the apartment.

"Just this guy. He, like…"

"It's disgusting."

Kirsten laughed. "You shouldn't talk."

"Would you shut up."

Kirsten glanced at me, and smirked. "Guess what she gave her boyfriend—"

"Don't," the other one shouted. "Don't you fucking dare!" She leaned over and tried to cover Kirsten's mouth.

"—her boyfriend for his birthday."

"Kirsten—Fuck!—don't."

Kirsten leaned over. Pushing the fat girl's hands off her face, she said, "Nude ones."

The fat girl collapsed back in her seat.

I added flames to Kris's mouth. The redhead sunk farther down in her chair.

"Did you?" I finally asked.

"You're such a fucking bitch Kirsten," she said, then to me, "Yeah. But only breast shots."

Alex did a twirl in the middle of the kitchen floor. She poured some of the freshly-made Tang and almost dropped the crystal tumbler.

"Alex. Be careful. That was your grand—"

"Sure mom," Alex said, walking toward me. "So, where's that guy you said was in the mental ward? You said he would come."

Damien sitting in the blue robe on the edge of the bed.

"Um," I said—there was something shiny in her tongue. "I don't know. I guess he's not coming."

"Anyway," she said and gulped all the Tang. "Let's go to my room."

In the family room kids watched David Lynch's *Lost Highway*, rewinding and re-watching the scene in which Dick Laurent forces Alice to strip at gun point. Marilyn Manson blared from the stereo. A boy around twelve screamed (off-key) the lyrics to "Cake and Sodomy."

We wove through the crowd and went into Alex's room. I sat on her bed. She closed the door and locked it.

"Aren't these cool?" She carried from her dresser a tray of white tea lights that her friends had bought her for her birthday. "Hey, do you want to see them?"

She lit nine or ten, then lowered the blinds and switched off the lights.

"Isn't this so cool," she said, standing with her face over the candles.

"Yeah. Really cool."

The two of us sat in silence, both of us staring at the eerie glow.

17

"Guess what I did on Tuesday?"

"I don't know."

She leaned forward, reaching behind her with both hands. When she lifted her black T-shirt, the bra came up with it. "See?" she said, her fingers straining to pull the material higher.

I didn't see—at least not at first. Then as Alex shook her torso, a tiny silver ring jiggled in one of the nipples.

"Yeah," I said.

"And this too," she said, sticking out her tongue.

"I noticed. Why'd you get it done?"

The expression on Alex's face changed. She lowered her T-shirt back over her breasts, reached around and refastened her bra.

"I don't know. I just wanted to," she said, staring at the floor.

"Isn't it, like, for oral sex?"

Alex looked at me surprised. "How did you know?"

"I don't know. Someone told me."

"I want to be someone's perfect bitch."

Feeling I should nod, I nodded.

"You know, my dad thinks you want to have sex with me."

"Really?"

"But he's kind of dirty himself. He cheated on my mom."

"That's not good."

Alex stood up and turned on the light. She blew the candles out in one breath and put the tray on the dresser.

"You know what we should do? We should like, fake we're having sex."

"Yeah?"

"Wouldn't it be cool?"

Before I could respond, she started. "Oh... *Oh...*" she groaned, contorting her face as if in extreme pleasure, "Yeah! Deeper! *Deeeeper!*"

Not sure of what I was supposed to do, I let out a perfunctory groan.

Alex stopped. "Come on! Louder!" she whispered.

We began again.

This time I tried to make the groans louder, more convincing, authentic, but at the same time, realized that doing this was even more embarrassing than if we were having sex.

Alex stopped, rolled over on her bed, knocked Grumpy Bear to the floor and howled with laughter. The laughter continued for a least a minute—I smiled while trying to think of a more appropriate response. Alex, sitting up and wiping tears from her eyes, said, "Let's see if anyone heard us."

I left shortly after that. On the way home I was frightened that I would start thinking things again. But when I got home *Taxi Driver* was on Bravo. I watched it and drifted off.

That night I slept soundly.

I hadn't planned to return to North Van that summer. My intentions had been to keep my apartment at UBC, work somewhere near the university during the day, and take a course at night. But the plan fell through when I discovered that the section I wanted was full. My aunt had offered to let me stay at the house in North Van, assuring me that she would be away most of the time. It would mean being on Kris's leash—financially that is—but I thought the chance to save four months' rent seemed worth whatever arguments we would have when she was around. Also, I was getting these strange thoughts in my apartment and didn't want to be there alone.

The morning following Alex's party I had an appointment with the doctor, but it wasn't till eleven. When I woke up I thought of Diane's small stomach bulge and the shape of her breasts in the T-shirt. I imagined my hand on her stomach and my fingers inched into the elastic waist band of her panties, my hand down inside them.

I was thinking of this when the phone rang.

The phone was still ringing when I finished. I got out of bed and hobbled down the hall awkwardly, my pyjama bottoms wrapped around my ankles. I crashed through the den door, got to the desk, and raised the phone with my left hand.

"Yeah. Hello."

There was a pause. "I called the business line, didn't I?" Kris's voice crackled with static.

"Sorry, I just got up," I said, still searching for Kleenex.

"You know I want you to—"

"I know I know," I said. "I forgot. I just got up."

Pause. If the connection were better I would've heard a sharp expulsion of air. I found a sheet of paper that didn't look important, and cradling the phone, wiped off my right hand.

"Anyway, how's the trip?" I asked. "Where are you?"

There was a long pause before Kris, speaking in a restrained tone, said that she was in San Francisco, actually San Jose—there had been some emergency and the plane had been rerouted. It had been unbelievably cold on the flight. They had run out of blankets and they had run out of white wine. The plane was an hour behind schedule—there had been a problem loading the luggage in Seattle—and they would probably lose more time before they reached L.A.

"Besides that," she said, "everything is just great!"

She asked if I had been keeping track of the messages, writing them down and erasing them from the answering machine so there would be room for more messages.

"I've written down a page," I said, lying.

"How many numbers?"

"I don't know. I don't have it."

"Where are you?"

"I'm on the portable. In the washroom."

"Oooookay…" she said. "Well, make sure you get them all. It's important."

"What day did you say you'll be home?"

She gave me the date and asked if I had made reservations for Harrison.

I tried to think what the safest answer would be.

"Trace!—I'll be furious if this is the first year we don't go to Harrison for the long weekend, and all because you can't—"

"Yeah, I know! I know!"

"Okay," she said. "I just want to make sure those reservations are made. How's UBC?"

"I finished."

"When?"

"Like, two weeks ago."

"How about money? Do you need me to put more into your account?"

"I'm okay."

"You sure? After L.A. I'm not sure when I'll be near a bank machine again.

"I'm fine."

"Just checking. I should go. I love you."

"I love you too."

After I hung up the phone, I called the hotel in Harrison and made the reservations for the Labour Day long weekend. Fortunately, there was still a vacancy. Each year we meet my other aunt and my cousin Emily at Harrison to spend some "family time." It's the only way, Kris says, she can tolerate them.

The messages on the machine were mostly from my friends. One from Alex inviting me to the party I'd just attended; two from Cam reminding me that he was returning on the 5th; a two-day-old one from Fahid (this guy who I hadn't spoken to in a year) telling me, "Quick, turn to 39. There's this documentary on Radiohead." And one more from Cam reminding me he was coming back. After I'd erased these, I replayed the ones for the company. The first message was from a man called Sun Young Lee— at least I think that's what his name was—and he said that he was interested in property in North Van, but only in the Handsworth catchment area. The second one was from Michael Daniels, this "associate" of Kris's. I recorded these in the notebook, then pressed erase.

When I went to the doctor's appointment that afternoon he said that things were fine. My blood work had come back and everything appeared to be normal.

When Damien had called near the end of May, he'd wanted me to guess where he was, and I'd thought of where he could be, then realized that it was a joke, a reference, an allusion to what he said the first time he called me from the psychiatric unit.

I hadn't heard from him again, and had assumed that he was out of the hospital. But a week after Alex's party, he called.

"Guess where I am?"

"Still?"

"I'm going to be out soon. Maybe another week or so. What are you doing tomorrow night?"

"Nothing. Do you want me to drop by?"

"Can you bring a six pack?"

"Are you allowed?"

"Get me whatever's on sale...Molson Canadian... TNT...whatever."

The next night, after stopping at the Cold Beer and Wine Store, I went to visit him. The evening was clear and warm, and it reminded me of the time I had previously visited him there, one year before. It had been the night he and I were supposed to be attending our grad.

I remembered the walk down the glassed-in corridor, the evening light grainy and soft filtering through the long bank of unwashed windows. I remembered being surprised that the nurse on duty that night—a *psychiatric* ward nurse—knew who my friend was. I remembered waiting in the lounge area, hearing glass breaking, joking to myself someone had gone crazy—not actually thinking anyone had gone crazy, just thinking someone had dropped something. I remembered Damien's mother running down the hallway, remembered her shouting, "He's broken the window! He's broken the window! Help—please!" And I remember the excitement I felt, and the guilt I felt later for feeling that excitement.

Damien was sitting on the edge of the bed, his headphones on. The music was loud and I could tell the song was Sabbath's "Paranoid." He banged his head in time with the music and slapped the drumbeat on his thighs. Around him on the bed were Slayer and Nirvana CDs, and on the bedside table, *An American Nightmare*, Jeffrey Dahmer's biography.

I was standing just inside the room when he noticed me. "Hey," he said. He turned off his Discman and pulled out the ear buds.

"Should you be reading this?" I said. I'd gone over and picked up Dahmer's biography.

"What?" He smiled sheepishly. "It's interesting."

I replaced the book.

"Are we going somewhere? I got the beer."

Damien got up, and took a bag of Drum tobacco and a Zippo lighter from his green jacket on the chair.

As I waited for him to stretch on the paper slippers they gave him in place of his shoes, I noticed his roommate standing by the window, a lanky guy about our age. He wore a purple tracksuit with its hood up and its sleeves pulled over his hands, and he appeared to be wearing black woollen mittens.

I nodded in greeting, but I don't think he saw me.

I was suspicious when Damien said he was allowed out of the hospital, but I didn't argue with him. When we got to the car, the beer was still cold. He cracked the first one open, and turned the radio to a station playing Young's "Cinnamon Girl."

When I glanced at him, I got the feeling he didn't want to talk.

The fresh leaves on the alders, the sun setting over the city, the amber skies greying—the evening was identical to that evening a year ago, and the idea that time never began and never ended came into my head.

"Have I showed you this?"

Take it easy, don't think about it.

"Trace?"

He held the Zippo with the Playboy insignia. "My dad got it in the duty-free, coming home from San Diego."

"Is he home now?"

"He's in Hawaii. Or maybe Maui, I can't remember."

The sun was shining in my face. I sighed, lowering the visor.

"Kris isn't home either."

"Where is—Are you okay?"

"What?" He was staring at me.

"Yeah—I don't know," I said, looking back at the sunset. *Take it easy*, I told myself. "Somewhere in the States, she's flying around looking at…" I shrugged. "Condos?"

"Are you going to have a party?"

I shook my head, then asked, "Who would I invite anyway?"

Damien didn't respond.

"Maybe we should invite your roommate."

"Vincent?"

"Is that his name?"

"Uh huh," he said and finished his beer. He set the empty can on the floor and pulled off another one.

"I bet he gets a lot of action."

Damien belched. "How about that girl you knew, the one that's really hot."

"Sadie? And do what? *Hey, Sadie*—" I made my voice sound dumb, "*Do you want to come by and hang out with me and my friend and listen to some old Nirvana CDs.*"

Damien burst out laughing—I felt better. The Zippo was lying by the gear shift and I picked it up. I ran my finger over the insignia, then flipped the lighter open and lit it.

"Here—don't waste the fluid."

I handed it back to him. "You talked to Cameron?"

He shook his head.

"He called me last week," I said. "He's coming back next month."

"So?"

Not sure why I'd mentioned it, I went back to looking out at the evening, watching the light fade on the city's glass towers.

Before we returned to the hospital, Damien drank another three cans. As I helped him stagger down the hall to his room, I was frightened that a nurse or someone would notice us. When we came into the room, 'Vincent' was still at the window—I got the feeling he hadn't moved once.

I helped Damien into bed and covered him with the blanket. As I started to leave he mumbled something.

"What did you say?" I said, leaning down.

"…I get out of the hospital, we'll go out."

"Sure," I said.

As I stepped back out into the twilight, I did whatever it took not to think. I gathered all the empty cans out of the car. A bus stop was nearby, and I jammed them in the trash receptacle attached to the pole. When I got back to the car, I lowered all the windows—even the ones in the back—and drove.

A few minutes later, I was racing along 15th Street to Grand Boulevard, then up the east side of Grand Boulevard, toward Lynn Valley. Damien's comments had got me thinking about Sadie. I'd met her the past fall at UBC, and there was a period around Christmas when I guess I was kind of obsessed with her. I would go over to her house two or three times a week and write essays for her women's studies classes, while she got ready to go clubbing with some guys who invariably were called

Mike or Steve or Brad. In the spring, we kind of fell out of touch, and I hadn't seen her since the end of term. But her house was close by, and when I reached the intersection with Mountain Highway I turned left on impulse, and started up the steep road.

I didn't expect her to be home, but the black Volkswagen her parents had bought her was in the driveway. I passed the house and turned left on Kilmer, and parked.

It was almost night. Vancouver twinkled over the dark treetops.

Her mother answered the door almost the moment I rang the bell. She was wearing the blue terry-towel track suit she always wore. "Tray," she said, mispronouncing my name. "Come in. How are you?" Her Slovakian accent made her hard to understand.

"Fine," I said. "Good. Is Sadie in?"

I stepped inside and leaned down to undo my laces.

"Sadie," she shouted, then turned back to me.

"Are you finished school?"

"Two weeks ago," I said.

"Sadie—she told me she finished the week before."

"Everyone has different exam schedules." I followed the mother into the front hall.

"I don't know. Sadie never tell us anything—Sadie!"

At the foot of the stairs I fiddled with my car keys. Dinner plates were still on the table in the kitchen and her father was watching a hockey game. The smell of Maggi sauce was in the air.

The woman started to call "Sadie" again, but Sadie was at the top of the stairs.

"What?" she shouted, then noticed me. "Trace. Did you tell me you were coming?"

"No. I was at the hospital."

She pouted—"Look at me."

I was—she was wearing a pink terry-towel tracksuit, her hair in curlers—actually, I preferred the look of her when she wasn't dressed up.

"You're fine," I said.

"Come up. I'm just getting ready."

In her room, I lay on the pink canopy bed while she sat at the matching bureau and finished her hair. The radio was on, playing "Go West" by the Pet Shop Boys.

Taped to the nightstand was a prayer written in Slovakian. Sadie'd told me her mother used to make her pray every night. Each time I was in the room, I'd try to figure out the pronunciation of the words.

Sadie, her back to me, hummed along with the song as she took curlers out of her hair. She had her hands raised over her head. *"There's this girl there, she's so fucking hot. She's kind of short? Blonde hair? Yeah—that's her!"* It was strange to think of the things guys said about her at UBC; now she was just a girl.

A few minutes passed without either of us speaking. I picked a *People* magazine off the floor and flipped past the glossy photos of Ricky Martin and Enrique Iglesias to the pages showing women.

"So, what were you doing at the hospital?" Sadie asked.

"A friend of mine, he—"

"Don't you think she's hot?" She pointed to the picture of Jennifer Lopez I'd turned to. "I mean, I'm not a lesbian. But she even turns me on." After that comment I didn't bother talking about Damien. I asked instead what she was doing tonight. She said not much, that she and some friends were getting together at the Avalon, that if I wanted to come, I could come, that there would probably be people from UBC there.

She took a black crushed-velvet top out of her closet. As I waited for her to return from the washroom, I paced the room and debated about whether I should go to Avalon. It would probably just make me feel lonely, but I wanted to go.

A beige bra hung off the back of the chair, and I bent down and examined it. I imagined her nipples pressed against the inside of the cups, and flipped the tag and read the measurements on the strap. 32 B. I repeated the number a couple of time trying to remember it.

It was strange—I could never really imagine Sadie having sex. I knew she had sex with guys, she was beautiful, and I was always seeing her in partial stages of undress, but when it came to the actual visuals, there was a blind spot.

Black and white model photos were wedged in the right side of the mirror frame, and I leaned forward to study them. They'd been taken when Sadie was fifteen, before she'd stopped growing and was told she was too short to model. When she told me, I'd remembered a quote by Hitler from the History 12 textbook: "the Czechoslovakians are a vile race of dwarfs." She looked happy in the photos.

Ten minutes later Sadie came back in the room. Before going to the washroom her face had been pale and featureless, like a young girl's. Now, with lip gloss, rouge and eyeliner, it looked like the faces in the magazine.

On the drive down to the club, I asked Sadie if she was going out with anyone and she said no. She had broken up with Steve just before the exams, and she wasn't going to date anyone for a while. She wanted to leave her summer open, she said. The drunken chant of Offspring's "Self Esteem" came on. She asked if she could change the station, and flipped to one playing Ace of Base's "All That She Wants."

At the Avalon there was quite a group of people—some I knew; some I didn't—and they'd pushed the tables together to form one long table. I sat down in what looked like an unoccupied chair, and Sadie sat next to me. As she'd predicted, people from UBC were there, and I waved at Hugh and Anna at the other end.

I was about to ask Sadie if she wanted anything to drink when I felt a hard tap on my right shoulder.

"That's *my* place." The guy was large, and bulky, and he wore a backwards Raiders hat and a down vest.

I tried to think of something to say.

"Leave—or I'll make you."

I went to the other end of the table to join Hugh and Anna and Paula. Hugh, whose real name was Hugo, and was either French and spoke Spanish or Spanish and spoke French—I couldn't remember—was dressed (as he always dressed) in light blue jeans (holes in the knees) a tweed jacket and a scarf; and he was talking to Anna, a Polish girl, who apparently modeled and who, when I met her the previous fall, had been going out with a guy called Bruce whom she'd said she loved and would marry and whom two weeks later she had to break up with—because she was in love with Hugh. As I sat down next to them I held out my hand for Hugh to shake. I guess he didn't see it. I turned to Anna and asked how her summer was going. "Great!" she shouted in a tone that suggested she hadn't heard what I'd said. She kept smiling and I couldn't think of another thing to say, so I said "Lemon," a word I once used to describe an English professor we both had and both disliked and which always made Anna laugh.

Anna laughed.

Hugh turned back to her and stroked her cheek and said something in… French? Spanish? English? Polish? At the other end of the table Sadie was on the lap of the guy who had told me to move. He massaged her thigh while flirting with the brunette across from him. Someone tapped my shoulder. It was Hugh. He shouted something, and after shouting it two more times, Anna told me that Hugh was wondering if I could get them two margaritas. As she said this, she patted my arm and smiled. At the bar, there was a crowd. It took me twenty minutes to get the drinks. Hugh and Anna had gone when I got back. When I found them, they were in the corner. I approached, I stopped.

Hugh's tweed coat was over Anna's lap, his hand was working under it. Anna's face had an earnest expression, her eyes half-glazed, her mouth half-open.

Back at the table, I drank the margaritas.

"Having fun?"

Paula was Chilean, and once told me that if she didn't shower everyday she got B.O.

"Uh—"

"I'll talk to you in a second," she shouted, getting up. "—gotta go pee."

The moment I got out to the parking lot, my mind cleared. The margaritas had done their job. The cold spring air felt good.

The club's sound system still thumping in my head, I drove up Keith Road, past the Catholic school I went to in junior high. A house beyond it had my aunt's real estate sign on its lawn.

On Lonsdale, I turned left. The highway led West, to Horseshoe Bay. I stamped the accelerator, lowered the front and back windows. All the stations that night were playing the Pet Shop Boys' "Go West"—I finally turned the radio off and put on Led Zeppelin's "Dazed and Confused...."

I pressed repeat.

The last week in May, I didn't do much. Each day I slept later and later, the thick blanket in the window stopping the sun from waking me. At first this had bothered me, my seeming purposelessness, but slowly I grew used to the rhythm of the days and the routine of killing time.

After the night at the Avalon I hadn't expected to hear from Sadie again—actually I didn't want to hear from her again. But she called the night before I was to pick Cam up from the airport. I was sitting on the sofa watching *Maniac* when the phone rang, and without pausing the movie, I grabbed the portable. "Patterson Realty," I said.

Her voice, after a pause, said, "I'm sorry. I think I have the wrong number."

"Sadie?"

"Trace? Why'd you say Patterson's Realty?"

I explained that it was my aunt's line and that was how she wanted me to answer it.

We asked each other about our breaks; and after a long story by Sadie about how she had quit Earl's and now worked at the Cactus Club and how her new manager was better than her old manager and how the new manager took her out for drinks, I asked, "So? Are you and—Brad—dating?"

"You mean Chad?"

"I guess. The guy at the Avalon."

"No—well, yeah. Yeah kinda."

"Really?" I said.

The movie was coming to my favourite scene. I held the phone away and covered the mouthpiece.

"Well, we're just seeing right now. I don't want to rush anything. I think that was the problem with Steve."

"Sure," I said.

On screen, Frank Zito (the maniac) leaped onto the hood of the parked car in which a couple had been frolicking. He held a hunting rifle and, crouching, taking careful aim, squeezed the trigger. The head of the driver exploded in slow motion, flinging brain and blood all over the woman's face.

"What's happening?" Sadie asked, sounding alarmed.

"What?"

"The screaming? Is someone hurt?"

"Oh, no," I said, imagining that the man in the car was Chad. I reached for the remote. "It's just some late night movie."

2

Cam's flight was late. To kill time I wandered the airport, went to the kiosks and through the souvenir stores, and got the impression of the city that a tourist might get—maple syrup, smoked salmon, totem poles, stuffed toy killer whales.

The girl I'd noticed earlier was still at the flight status screens when I returned, and I went up beside her. She was about my age—maybe nineteen or twenty—she had an olive complexion, and hair that was thick and wavy and black. She stood patiently, holding her black leather handbag at waist level with both hands, a purple cardigan draped over her right arm. The dress she wore was white with black orchid prints, and there were copper medallions on her brown leather sandals.

As I stood beside her, I took furtive glances while pretending to study the computer terminals. Her demeanour and clothing suggested that she wasn't from here, and that fact, for some reason, made it easier for me to speak to her.

"Are you waiting for someone from Mexico?" I said finally.

My voice was weak and I started to repeat the question. But a smile was already there. "Yes, yes, *Me he co*."

The smile remained and I felt encouraged to say more. I forced a grin. "My friend. He's coming from Mexico."

"Yes? He from *Me he co*?" she said. She had obviously misunderstood and thought Cam was *from* Mexico.

The strap of the blue bra was visible beneath the white dress strap. I looked back at her face. "Are you staying in Vancouver?" I asked.

"Yes, studying English."

"You like it?"

"Yes. It very nice."

"I'm Trace," I said. I held out my hand, and she shook it, her hand soft and cool. "My name Maria," she said.

We said one or two more things.

Then, afraid of freaking her out by asking for her number, I offered mine.

She seemed enthusiastic. She took an agenda from her handbag. As I waited for her to open it and get a pen, I tried to guess the size of her breasts under the dress's material.

"O. Kay," she said carefully.

I gave her my number. She wrote it on one of the pages, and I noticed her chipped nail polish. She looked up at me. Her eyes were very dark brown.

"I. Will. Call." she said, concentrating hard on the pronunciation of each word.

She waved to someone coming through the door, then turned to me and said—this time a bit faster, "I. Will. Call."

Cam came through the doors, wearing a sombrero, and so tanned he looked black. As always, he had the hulking posture and the intense glare that had frightened people in high school.

I had to shout twice before he saw me. When he did, his expression softened.

"Hola," I said.

"Mr. Patterson, Mr. Patterson," he said, shaking his head with a sort of sad/happy disbelief. "Long time no see." He held out his hand and I put mine in it, and he squeezed hard.

We didn't say anything else till we reached the end of the railing that separated us.

"Can you watch this?" He handed me his grey duffle bag. "I got to use the washroom. Those fuckers in customs wouldn't let me go."

The duffle bag was the one he'd taken to outdoor school in Grade 11. I had a clear memory of that period, but at the same time, the memory seemed distant.

When Cam returned, I pointed at the bag and asked him if he remembered outdoor school.

"Oh. Yeah," he said, obviously thinking of something else.

"Trouble with customs?"

"Fuck! I was *this* close," Cam said, indicating a few millimetres with his thumb and index finger, "to punching the bitch in the head."

He picked up the duffle bag. I started toward the parking lot and he followed. "Is there a number you can call to complain about those people?"

"I guess."

"They took away my tequila."

"All of it?"

"Except one bottle."

"Isn't that all you're allowed?"

"I really wanted to punch that bitch in the mouth."

When we stepped through the doors, the early June heat wave hit us like a wall. We crossed the road and went through the parkade and out again into the hot bright sunlight. A plane roared by overhead.

By the time we reached the BMW we were sweating.

"Nice car."

"It's my aunt's." The leather seat was burning and I slid forward and tried to keep my bare thighs off the seat.

"Crank the air conditioner."

"I did," I said, and shifted into reverse.

A mile from the airport Cam's mood improved. Air-drumming along with the Chili Peppers on the stereo, he said for the sixth time that he couldn't believe he was back.

"So, tell me a story, Mr. Patterson. What's been happening?"

"Not much. Just going to some parties," I said. "By the way, I saw Damien."

"Damien!" Cam slapped the top of the door and glared at me. "Fuck! Don't tell me you still hang around with *that* loser."

"Shouldn't I?" I said, pretending not to know what was coming next.

"The loser fucking totalled my car."

Cam, for some reason, always blamed Damien for the accident we were involved in.

I didn't say anything more, and we were downtown before he asked, "So tell me, has he put his life back together again?"

"He had to spend some time in A2 again. Some problem with his meds."

"I bet you liked that."

"What do you mean?" I said.

But Cam only laughed and said, "Don't worry. Forget it."

Cam's parents had sold their house in North Van when he was in Mexico and now lived in the Properties. As I started the maze of roads up the mountain, the city falling away behind us, I asked, "So why'd they move?"

"I don't know," Cam said staring out the window. "My father made a bunch of money on some land deal or something."

"Is that a bad thing?"

"I guess not."

We didn't speak again until we arrived at the house. The houses across the road were down the hill and over their roofs I could see Vancouver from the tip of the UBC endowment lands in the west to Burnaby Mountain in the east. But Cam's parents' house, like a lot of houses in that area, had a shabbiness to it, and if I had my back to the view and ignored the Mercedes and Range Rovers in the neighbours' driveways, I'd assume it was worth a tenth of its value.

"Well, I guess that's it," Cam said. "I'd invite you in, but..."

"Sure."

"We'll do something this weekend."

"Sure," I said.

"Thanks for picking me up at the airport."

"No problem."

"What was he even doing there?"

"What do you mean?"

"You know—where he was?"

"Mexico?"

"Mmm," Damien said, gulping the end of his beer. It was Friday night and he and I were sitting in The Bourbon, a bar in Gastown where college students went to slum. We were supposedly there "to celebrate" his release from the psych ward.

"I mean, what was he doing in fuckin' Mexico?"

"I think he expected to meet some women," I said, gazing at the circling bodies. The counter we sat at ran along the long edge of the dance floor.

"What?"

"He *Expected. To. Meet. Latin. Women.*"

Damien sneered. He took a drink and said, "Why'd he go there? There's enough here."

He gestured with his head to the dance floor. I didn't know what he was talking about, then saw an East Indian girl in a purple tube top and realized that that was his idea of a Latin woman.

Damien shouted something.

"Say that again."

"—hope he gets bit by a fucking scorpion."

"Why?" I asked, laughing. "Do you hate him?"

Damien didn't answer. He downed the remaining beer and told me to guard his stuff while he used the washroom.

I sipped my drink and watched the dance floor. It was crowded with dancers, but all of them danced in loose groups or alone—none of them danced in pairs. I thought about why I had mentioned Cam's arrival and realized that I guess I had hoped they would repair their friendship now that they were out of high school. Why this was important to me, I didn't know.

Two middle-aged women circled toward the counter. They'd beckoned me and Damien to join them earlier, and I waited to see if they would repeat the invitation. The one with the rhinestone top was staring in my direction, but she didn't seem to see me.

A few feet from her, there was another person I'd noticed before. He was about my age, but he had this immense afro that made him look like someone from the '70s. All night he'd been attempting to dance with someone. He would keep going up, and keep trying to join the circles of dancers. But each time the circle closed without him.

He had now moved close to a woman in a white halter top and the woman, without losing sync with the beat, turned her shoulder to him, then her back.

"What I Like About You," was just fading out when Damien returned. He was carrying a pitcher of beer. He started to pour some into my glass.

"I can't. I got to drive."

Damien shrugged, and filled his own glass. He pulled out the bar stool and sat on it.

"So why do you hate Cam?" I shouted.

The guy with the afro was directly in front of us. He tried casually to attach himself to another circle of women as the circle closed without him.

"What?" Damien yelled, craning his head toward me.

But I didn't get a chance to repeat the question. The afro kid had his hands on the brass rail in front of us, then his foot.

"Hey! *Hey!*" Damien yelled, holding his hands out to stop the guy. But the guy catapulted himself over the counter, catching the pitcher with his knee.

Beer was everywhere.

I had pushed back in time to avoid it running on my legs, but Damien's jacket was soaked. "Fuck," I thought I heard Damien say as he stood up. He was facing the afro boy, his back to me. I couldn't hear what he was saying, but the afro kid looked down, his arms hanging loose at his sides.

A group of four men stood behind the afro kid, watching. Though the music was too loud to hear anything, I was certain that someone was chanting, "Fight, fight, fight."

Damien held his jacket up, shaking it. He pointed at it and the kid said something, nodding.

After what seemed like a long time, Damien turned to me. "Let's fucking go."

The cold night air was a relief. A line up of people stood waiting to enter. The doorman, glancing at us as we came out the door, I guess noticed the expression on Damien's face. "Is everything alright, gentlemen?"

Damien stopped. "Look what this fuckin' asshole did to my jacket."

The man leaned closer, and the specks of dandruff became visible on his black dress shirt.

As Damien started to explain, the people in the line-up watched. The dirty blond with the red poodle skirt had bare legs that ended in Dorothy-from-*The-Wizard-of-Oz* ankle socks and I was staring at those legs when Damien said, "And he threatened me with a fuckin' knife?"

The doorman's eyes looked like they were going to fall out. "A knife?" he asked, incredulous.

"Yeah, a knife," Damien said, his tone so earnest that even I believed him.

"Where? What does he look like?"

The description Damien gave, fortunately, wasn't too accurate; he described the guy as having dreadlocks. He gestured with his head to where we'd been sitting, and the man, leaning forward and pointing, said, "There?"

Damien nodded.

"Okay, thanks." He patted Damien on the shoulder. "Can I get you another drink?"

"We're fine," I said.

"You sure?'

I assured him we were.

"I'm really sorry this happened. Come again, guys. Next time I'll make sure you get free drinks."

We thanked him and left.

I'd parked the car on Robson. As we started back, Damien and I were silent. The streets looked how they always looked after you left a club, cold and deserted. It must have rained when we were in the bar because everything had a fresh shine to it.

When we turned onto Seymour Street, Damien said "Sorry dude, sorry dude," making his voice sound like a stoner's. "Sorry dude, Sorry dude—*Fuck!*"

"Is that what he said?"

"Fucking hippie."

"He didn't have a knife, did he?"

As if in explanation Damien said, "Look what he did to my jacket." He held up the coat, the Manchester United windbreaker his dad bought for him in England.

"A brand new fucking jacket, and some Rastafarian dumps beer on it."

We were almost at the car when Damien said, "Just one more beer."

"You sure?"

"Just one."

We checked one place—that bar wanted five dollars to enter. The next club was the same. When we finally found a bar without a cover charge, it was a café on

Burrard Street. There was a group of young men in the fenced section under the canopy, but inside the café it was deserted. The woman behind the counter was olive-skinned, and was so short only her elfish face showed above the glass. Damien ordered the pitcher special and I asked for steamed milk. When I placed my order, the young woman made a cute expression. I tried to think of something witty to say to her as she prepared the orders.

"I should have wasted that fucker," Damien said.

"Yeah, you should have," I said, watching the woman froth the milk with steam.

"But I didn't, did I?"

"No, you didn't," I said.

When we were seated, Damien asked, "Why did I even order this?" and pointed at the pitcher.

"Because you're an alcoholic," I said. I began to laugh, but stopped, noticing the expression on his face.

"Sorry," he said. "We'll go soon. I probably won't even finish this."

"Whatever."

He showed me his jacket again and said, "I should have wasted that fucker."

"Uh huh." My eyes followed the server as she wiped the counter with a cloth and washed the cloth and wrung it out.

"But I'm so controlled. I mean, isn't that the most controlled thing you can do, a guy spills beer all over your jacket and you're like cool about it? One of the guys standing there said, 'Man, I would've wasted the guy,' but I didn't, right? I just stayed cool. Now that's controlled, isn't it? Right, Trace? Right?"

"Uh huh."

The server was now on the lap of one of the guys under the canopy outside. He'd passed her a hand-rolled cigarette—or maybe a joint—and I wondered if she knew them, or if they'd just invited her to join their group.

"That's controlled, isn't it?"

"That's controlled," I said, wishing that I knew the answer.

"Anyway, I'm almost finished," Damien said, dumping the last of the beer into the schooner.

The bubbles on the top of the foam in the pitcher started to pop.

By the time we got back to his place, he'd want more. That, and to listen to the cassette tapes we made of our band when we were sixteen. He kept them in a shoebox by his ghetto blaster, and when we stayed up late drinking, he brought them out and said how good we were, how we should have played Seylynn Hall, how *we* could have been Nirvana.

And if I had been Kurt Cobain...

To save money Kris had flown into Seattle (instead of Vancouver) and taken the bus. It was due in at Pacific Central at about nine.

On the way to meet her, I stopped by Sadie's house. She was sitting on her bed when I came in her bedroom, cutting split ends out of her hair and watching television. "Men are *so* fucked up," she said. I was tempted to ask her who fucked them up, but instead asked if she was still going out with Brad, but she said I meant Chad (whom I think was the boyfriend after Brad) and no, she wasn't going out with him anymore because he'd cheated on her, that her friends caught him downtown with this Asian girl.

"I mean, the girl had these piercings," Sadie said, shaking her head in disbelief.

I shook my head too.

Ricky Martin came on TV, and Sadie said how handsome he was. She loved how he dressed. Guys never dressed like that in Vancouver, and if they did, they'd be accused of being gay. She also said that he said the sweetest thing to this fan. When the fan asked him what his favourite type of woman was, the description he gave was exactly the fan's description.

"I mean, isn't that so sweet?"

"Sure," I said.

Her mother came in the room, and she and Sadie began to argue in Slovakian. I listened for five minutes, then lied and said that I wasn't feeling well.

As I stepped down the cement front steps, I thought, "And this is the girl I'm obsessed with?"

Crossing Second Narrows that evening I looked to my right and saw below the dusk skies the downtown core, sparkling. The scene of it reminded me of a movie I'd seen when I was nine. It was about a stalker that kills this woman in Connecticut, and returns four years later to kidnap her son and the father's new girlfriend. He takes the pair downtown and holds them hostage in this room under Grand Central Station. All the commuters passing through the station have no idea what's going on under it. I didn't remember much else about the plot but the images from the movie had stuck in my mind, probably because I'd been the same age as the boy. I'd watched in on the old TV that used to be in the den, one of those sets from the 50s, with the angled legs, and I remembered feeling cozy and safe in the house in North Van, in the suburbs, all the lights out and the room bathed in blue light from the screen, but excited by the idea that the city was out there. Waiting.

Pacific Central, the building where Kris's bus was arriving, used to be the Canadian National Railway terminal. As I pulled into its parking lot I noticed that the illuminated yellow letters on the station's roof now spelled PACIFIC CENTRAL. Inside, the waiting room was brightly lit. The high gilded ceiling and the patterns on it looked to me about the same as when my grandfather had taken me down there and shown them to me. But the station clock and the skylight seemed to be new additions.

I walked to the gate leading to the train platform—beyond the glass there were silver passenger cars—then headed for the far end of the station. A sign read "BUSES" and I stepped outside onto the platform. The air was cold out there, and even though it was summer, it felt with the dampness almost like fall.

Back inside the station, I noticed a guy about my age alone on one of the benches, holding a khaki duffle bag on his lap. He wore a plaid shirt and hiking boots. He looked strong and confident. He returned my stare, and I looked away. The only other person in the room was a native Indian who was at the ticket booth.

I wandered back to the other end of the station and seeing the washroom, went inside. I didn't really have to use the toilet, but I slipped into a stall and clicked shut the door and squatted on the toilet seat. There was something about enclosed spaces that I found comforting. The three blue walls around me a sort of protection.

I tried to urinate, but nothing came. Graffiti was scrawled into the paint in front of me:

No more, immigration, No more!
Die Racist Pig
My little cock can go where big cocks can't
In my bum
Fag

Still squatting on the seat, I shifted my weight to my left hip and spreading my legs, set down my right hip. When I leaned forward, my ass spread under me—this is what they must do, I thought.

While I sat there, a couple of men entered the washroom. One of them said something in a curt tone and I tried to hear the other's response. Whatever he said was lost in the echo—maybe they weren't even speaking English.

Now there was the loud echoing hiss of a man pissing.

I imagined what it would be like if the men started shaking the door, or threatening me, or if they came in and raped me.

Water rushed from a faucet. An electric dryer roared. Someone said something and footsteps faded. Then it was silent except for the churning of a ventilator.

When I returned to the waiting room, a man who I thought was a security guard followed me. I stood by the curtained hole in the marble wall where the train luggage was unloaded on a conveyer belt, keeping the guard in the corner of my eye. I was waiting for him to approach me or speak to me.

He cleared his throat and left.

Aunt Kris described the "horrors" of her trip as I drove her and her "travel companion" Steve back to North Van—how every flight they took was delayed, how the toilets weren't working, how passengers (some of whom were very elderly) weren't even given blankets. She said that they didn't have a chance to eat in Seattle, and that she and Steve were famished and wanted to eat before they got home.

"Is Earl's alright?" I asked as I turned onto the Georgia Street viaduct.

"Fine. Anywhere. It doesn't matter," she said, pulling a package of cigarettes from her handbag. "Don't look at me. This trip was enough to make anyone start again."

She rolled down the window and described the second leg of the journey. Back east she decided to take the train between New York and Washington. To begin with, she hated New York, way too many buildings, and the trip to Washington was horrible. She had gone to use the washroom and found that someone had written his name on the mirror in shit. And then—

"Earl's?" Kris asked when we pulled into the parking lot. She said this as if were unthinkable.

"I thought you said it didn't matter?"

"But I didn't think—Okay. Fine."

When we got inside there was a line-up. As we waited, Kris let out loud exasperated sighs and checked her watch compulsively. I tried to ignore this by studying the waitresses. All were very young and very blond, and all dressed in skin-tight black slacks and T-shirts. They moved earnestly about the foyer, taking reservations and seating people, and I remembered what Sadie'd told me about working here—they only hire pretty young girls and tell each of them that Earl's is a stage and they must always be performing.

When we were finally seated, Kris and Steve ordered white wine and asked me if I was drinking anything. I felt like beer, but said, "Water's fine." I didn't want to invite one of Kris's caustic comments about me becoming an alcoholic.

While she and Steve argued about whether to have dynamite rolls or Caesar salads, I noticed that Steve was more tanned than when he'd left, that his linen shirt and his cotton pants looked new and that his blond hair was lighter. I flashed on an image of him mounting Kris in a hotel room and shook my head, trying not to think about it.

A girl with dirty blonde hair and satin choker brought Kris and Steve the glasses of wine, and when she set the drinks on the table, I realized that I knew her. She had been in my English class in high school. She'd been interested in literature and writing poetry and hadn't seemed like the type of girl who would work here. When she noticed me looking at her, she gave what seemed like a reluctant grin. But I wasn't sure if she actually remembered me, or if it was part of 'the performance.'

After we ordered and Kris finished her first glass of wine, she ordered a second.

"So, how's your summer been? Have you been able to survive without your old Kris to take care of you?" she said, and laughed.

"Fine."

"And school?"

"I'm finished."

"It's only June."

"I've been finished since April."

"And you didn't take summer courses?"

I didn't know what to say, then remembered that as part of our agreement I was supposed to be working for her.

"Wouldn't Revenue Canada get suspicious?"

She shook her head as if disgusted.

"What?" I said.

"Nothing." Her face brightened as the waitress handed her a second glass of wine.

When the girl had left, I said, "What? What did you want to say?"

Kris shook her head and looked down, grimacing. "Nothing. I'm just curious."

Steve was leaning back in the booth, looking around the restaurant like he didn't know what was going on.

"What do you want to say?"

Kris glared at me. "I think *we* know."

"What?"

"Patterns—that's what we are talking about, Trace, patterns."

I'd expected for her to make this vague insinuation about her sister and my father, and told myself to ignore the comment, to pretend that she hadn't said it. But I could feel the jittery feeling come back into my arms, the feeling I'd been trying to push down for the past three or four weeks. Suddenly it seemed very dark outside the windows.

Kris took a sip of her wine and twisted the bracelet on her left wrist. Steve checked his watch. He put his arm up over the back of the booth and stared off in the distance. The waitress with the choker passed our table.

"Hi."

I must have sounded weird, because she looked startled. She quickly recovered the smile though and asked, "Is everything okay?"

"Do you have martinis?"

"Okay, I'll bring you the list."

"I'll just have a gimlet?"

"Sorry—what was—"

"A gimlet. Just gin and lime juice."

"Oh. Okay. I'll ask the bartender."

After she left, Kris said, "Patterns, Trace, patterns."

When the gimlet arrived, I expected Kris to stop me, to tell me that I was the designated driver, or that I was becoming an alcoholic like my father. She didn't.

She let me order one gimlet after another.

And when it was time to go home, we had to order a taxi, and she and Steve helped me into the backseat.

The hour hand was almost at one. I raised my head and waited for the headache. When there wasn't one, I sat up. I ran my tongue around my mouth and over my teeth. My teeth had a fuzzy film on them and my mouth was dry and tasted sour. Sometime in the night I had vomited, and there was a small stain on the rug by the closet. (There'd been red specks in it, and I'd panicked thinking that I was bleeding internally; before realizing that the specks were pieces of red pepper.)

No one was in the kitchen. I poured myself milk using one of the McDonald's glasses I had collected with my grandparents as a child; and leaning against the fridge, chugging the drink, I imagined me standing there as a scene in a film, like Malcolm McDowell drinking "milk-plus."

A cool breeze blew through the open patio door, and I put the glass in the sink and went outside.

When I caught sight of Kris, she was lying on the chaise longue on the far side of the pool, tanning, her arm covering her eyes. Her mouth was half-opened, and her two top front teeth seemed more bucked than they normally did. As I sat on the grass beside her, I noticed that her breasts seemed larger than the last time I saw them, the nipples darker and more wrinkled.

On the table next to her was a pack of Matinée Special Mild, a Danielle Steele novel, and a glass of white wine.

"Hi," I said.

Squinting, she looked at me.

"Oh, you *decided* to get up," she said and covered her eyes again.

"Aren't you going to cover up?"

A loud sigh. "If it bothers you that much." She reached for her polo shirt. "I swear, you're as prudish as your grandparents were." she said and draped the shirt across herself. "Who would think that Jack was your father?"

"Where's Steve?"

"Out. Golfing, I think. Are you going to mow the lawn later?"

"If you want."

"That would be nice. How do you feel?"

"Not bad. A bit weak."

"Now if you were Jack, you'd start drinking again."

"I can't imagine that."

"Give it time."

I turned to the house, but then asked, "Where? Where would he start? At home?"

"No. He never drank around your mother. He would go to some expensive hotel downtown and drink—the hypocrite. He would never pay for your mother to go first class or to stay in the penthouse when they went on holidays. But when he went drinking it had to be the best. There probably isn't a good hotel downtown he didn't stay in, the Hotel Vancouver, the Bayshore. All Jess had to do was call the most expensive hotels to find him. And he wouldn't go dancing or to the dining room or the lounge—you know, what people normally do when they stay at an expensive hotel—he would just sit in his room and drink himself shit-faced, pass out, then wake up and drink some more. He could have done it in a Super 8.

"Then two or three days later he would call Jess—I can't believe I'm related to such a stupid woman—he would call and see if the waters were calm, and that stupid sister of mine would forgive him and he would come home and be nice for the next month or so, and then do it again.

"And it always happened during a full moon—you should check if last night was a full moon—and Jess and I would make plans for that weekend, because we knew he was going to go on one of his benders, and we would go with other friends and on dates and then wait for him to call."

I waited for more.

"Anyway, if you're not going to say anything, please leave. I don't want tan lines" she said, taking off her top.

On Saturday Alex had another party. After an hour, I was bored and decided to go home.

I was half out the door when I remembered my trench coat. Alex had put it in her parents' bedroom. When I went in there to get it, I found Diane propped against the headboard, smoking a cigarette and drinking a glass of wine. The bedside lamp was on, and a bottle of red sat next to it.

"Sorry. Don't mind me. I am just taking a break," she said, looking as if she were about to cry.

"Do you want me to leave?" I said, backing toward the door.

"No. It's okay. Just come in. Shut the door behind you. I don't want any of *them* in here."

I closed the door.

"Here. Sit down." She leaned forward to move my coat from the foot of the bed, and I sat down.

She took a long drag off her cigarette, and held it in while studying me, then exhaled.

"You must think this is terrible."

"What?"

She waved her hand in a semi-circle. "This!"

"You mean the party?"

"The *party.* The *kids—everything.*"

"Um, no. Not really. I think it's kind of—interesting."

"Yeah," she said, smiling wanly. "Interesting! That's a good word. Letting my daughter and all her friends get stoned at my house—I bet your aunt wouldn't be allowing this to happen."

I coughed. "At least you're supervising them, right?"

"Supervising. There's another good word." She took a drag of the cigarette and exhaled. "I like you. You make me feel better about myself. You make me feel like I'm a *responsible* adult." She picked up the wine glass. "She raised you?" she asked.

"Who—Kris?"

Diane, taking a sip, nodded.

I shook my head. "I was with my grandfather. Until he got sick a few years ago."

"Is he in a home now?"

"No—both of them are dead."

"Here, do you want some? Sorry I don't have another glass, but just take a sip from the bottle." She held it out to me.

"No. Really it's okay."

"No. Drink some. It will help you keep *those demons* at bay. You're making me feel like some kind of alcoholic."

"What do you mean?" I said.

"Drinking alone, you make me feel like some kind of alcoholic."

"No. The other thing."

She looked at me confused.

"Demons," I said.

"Oh! The *demons*," she laughed. "You know—those pesky thoughts. Those voices telling you you're nothing. Your husband climbing into bed with your sister, your daughter's a slut—don't you hear those voices?"

I quickly shook my head.

"*Of course not*," she said, sounding almost bitter. She took a drag off the cigarette.

A boy outside the door yelled, "Ozzy's god!"

"So… are you and Alex sleeping together?"

"Uhh…"

"Never mind. Don't answer. I shouldn't have asked. It's really none of my business. I think it's great Alex is going out with you. You'll certainly treat her better than a lot of guys. Some of the people at this party." She shook her head.

"And if the two of you are having sex—no—please don't say anything. I know Alex is responsible and she's using protection, so I'm not worried. Though I think it a bit strange that a guy your age wants to hang out with all these kids."

She drained her glass of wine and refilled it. She offered me the bottle.

This time, I took it. I took a big drink and handed it back to her.

"No. You finish it. I shouldn't have anymore. After all, I have to be the 'responsible adult,'" she said, using her fingers to indicate the quotation marks.

I took two large gulps, and finished the bottle.

She got up and opened the door. I retrieved my coat and followed her. A group of kids stood near the door, and as we passed them, one stared at me. He had a "My name is" sticker on his T-shirt, and it said that his name was "Satan." When I turned my back, one of them mumbled, "Motherfucker," and I was certain that it was him.

Though I'd spent the last week avoiding her, I found myself wishing Kris was home when I returned from the party. The wine hadn't had much effect, and the house was dark and looked ominous set back from the road behind a row of hemlocks and towering spruces. I walked quickly up the driveway, and after two failed attempts, jabbed my key in the lock.

As I stepped in the foyer I was struck by how the scene would appear in a slasher film. The viewer, taking the perspective of the killer in the master bedroom, would see my figure appear down the hall in the distance. A dissonant synthesizer chord would suggest his deranged state.

I slipped off my loafers, and turned on each light I passed on the way to the kitchen. I fixed a gin and tonic. In the living room, I put *Dark Side of the Moon* on the turntable.

It was in the middle of "Time" (and my second gin and tonic) that the phone rang. I sat there listening to the ring, waiting for the answering machine to cut in. Then realized that even if it was one of Kris's clients, I wanted to hear someone's voice.

"Patterson Reality," I slurred. I giggled, covering the mouthpiece, and waited for a reply.

Silence.

I looked down the hall toward the master bedroom. Someone started laughing hysterically on the phone. The laughter stopped. "Traeee. This is Sadie. I'm sooo horny. And my double penetration anal vibrator is broken. And I was just wondering if maybe you could cooome over and Pen neeee trate me." It was a male voice imitating a female's.

"Damien?"

He began to laugh again.

As I waited for him to stop, I picked up a memo pad and sketched a beard around Kris's face. She started to look like Charles Manson, and I added a swastika to her forehead.

"Guess where I am?" Damien finally said.

"You're joking."

He laughed.

"You were just there."

"Cool, eh?"

"Wait a second. Let me change phones."

After I got the portable from the study, I returned to the living room and turned down the volume on the stereo. "You're joking, right?"

"Nope."

"You were just there."

"They found the bodies, the severed heads, the—"

"Seriously."

'I *am* serious."

I didn't respond.

"I'm serious," he said and started laughing again.

I put the phone on the coffee table and finished the gin and tonic. When I picked up the phone again, he was saying, "—changing my meds again. The last ones were making me sleepy. They're going to try something different. They think it will make me feel better. There might be side effects so they want to monitor me."

I heard someone shout in the background.

"Got to go. Bring some beer."

Before I could say "Yes" or "No" he'd hung up.

I don't know what medication they put Damien on, but when I went to visit him the following evening he was a different person. For most of our visit he lay on the bed and stared up at the ceiling. When I asked him something, he either just remained silent, or answered in monosyllables. At one point I got so bored I picked up the biography of Jeffrey Dahmer and paged through it. In the middle, there was a picture of Dahmer as an infant, and I could imagine him getting excited for presents at Christmas, and decorating jack-o'-lanterns at Halloween.

Near the end of the visit Damien took me out to the cafeteria, where he pointed out this middle-aged black woman with sagging breasts, and asked me if I didn't think she was hot.

It was nine when I left hospital. The sun was gone, there was a pink afterglow in the West. I didn't feel like going home.

For about an hour I drove aimlessly around North Van, down Lonsdale—along Marine Drive, past grain elevators on the low road and up Third Street—all the while trying not to lose it. The strategy that I had used since childhood to deal with life was failing me. The effort to see myself in a movie was becoming increasingly difficult, and the real story was looming into view. Damien's trips to the psychiatric ward weren't scenes out of *One Flew Over the Cuckoo's Nest* or an image from a Green Day video. For the first time, they were assuming their true reality: a sad beginning to what would probably be a sad life.

But I poured all my attention on the road ahead of me. The radio began to play one good song after another, and I was able to avoid whatever I had started to feel.

When I finally got tired, it was around ten. The feeling that this was all a scene in a film was again there—at least for the time being—and I headed to the video store and rented *The Little Girl Who Lives Down the Lane* and the first *Friday the 13th,* before heading home.

When I got there, there was a message on the answering machine.

It took five listens, but finally I was able to decipher that the caller—a woman called Maria—was the girl from the airport.

3

THE GABLED HOUSE was the third one in from the Drive. I checked the number I'd copied down again and shoved the scrap of paper into my pocket and unlatched the gate.

As I went through the yard and climbed the stairs and rang the doorbell, I still couldn't believe that the girl had called.

I was watching the sway of a woman's breasts on the opposite side of the street when the door opened behind me. I turned. Facing me was a man in his late twenties, very thin, dark-looking, scruffy.

"Hi. Is Maria here?"

"Uh." He scratched his head. "Maria. Just moment."

"Maria," he shouted into the house. He wore an Argentinian football jersey, and his narrow face had a day's growth of whiskers.

After a woman's voice upstairs yelled back something in Spanish, he turned to me and said, "She changing. Come in."

The living room was through an archway on the left, and I sat on one of the two threadbare sofas and looked at the high ceiling and the worn wood floors and a photo of a white family on the mantel. Something hit the floor

65

in a room upstairs. The voice of a man passing outside shouted, "What I told him is—." A grey cat meandered into the room, looked at me, left.

I was still trying to remember if Maria was good-looking when I heard footfalls on the stairs. She entered the room. The blue jeans looked tight on her. She wore with them a blue tank top and blue suede flip-flops on her feet. She was fatter than I remembered.

"'ola," she said leaning down, and kissed my right cheek.

"Hola," I said. I stood up.

I followed her out to the foyer where she picked up a small black handbag. The man who answered the door now reappeared. He said something in Spanish, and she slapped his shoulder and he laughed.

It took me awhile, because Maria's English wasn't very good, but I found out on the drive downtown that the family who owned the house had rented it to international students while they toured Europe. Maria, Fernando (the guy who answered the door) and two Japanese women were staying there.

When I asked her if she liked Fernando, she laughed.

Downtown, I wanted to know what Maria wanted to do, and she said she didn't know and we ended up walking through the crowd of late-afternoon tourists on Robson Street.

Every few feet Maria stopped to push her flip-flops back on her feet and when she did this the third time, I asked her if they were too small, and she told me that she'd washed them and—here she stopped and gestured with her hands that they'd become small.

"You mean shrunk? " I said and imitated her gesture.

"What?"

"Shrunk—you know—got smaller?" But, of course, as I said this, I realized she didn't know.

"What's da word?"

"Shrunk."

She repeated the word three times, then took out her notebook and wrote the word in it.

After we'd walked for a time, I became nervous. I felt certain that people were looking at us and that someone was going to stop us.

When we passed the clothing store Jacob, Maria said she wanted to go in and I followed her through the aisles. In lingerie, she stopped and held up a pair of transparent lacy panties.

I pretended not to notice.

"Do you want me to wait outside?" I asked.

She glanced at me with a concerned expression on her face.

"I go outside," I said, pointing.

"Okay," she said, nodding.

I walked down the aisle, but she followed me. She must have thought I was telling her I wanted to go.

We walked another block without saying one word, then she asked, "Are you desperate with me?"

I thought at first that she was talking about sex, but realized that this couldn't be what she meant, that what she was asking about was her English.

"No," I said, laughing.

"Why you laugh?" she asked. I thought about telling her what "desperate" meant in English, but realized that I wouldn't be able to explain.

At the corner of Robson and Hornby, I asked Maria if she would like to see the exhibits at the Vancouver Art Gallery.

"Yez. Pleaze."

In the line-up she told me that she'd painted in Mexico. Her mother owned a small ceramics factory and that she worked for her.

Just before the admissions desk, she wanted to know if she should pay. I asked her what couples did in Mexico, and she said that the man pays, so I paid the eighteen dollars.

On the third floor there was an exhibition of Warhol's silkscreens, one of Elvis Presley and four electric chairs. In high school I had liked Warhol and wanted to be like him, in the centre of things without being affected by them.

In another part of the gallery there was a large photograph of a woman masturbating. Maria studied the picture, and I wondered if she was becoming aroused by it, or just disgusted.

When we returned to the house it was empty and Maria asked if I would like to come upstairs. We went to her room on the second floor. I sat on her bed. She took a cream-coloured photo album from a shelf and sat beside me. Inside the album were photos of her mother's ceramics factory and of her brothers, and Maria's modeling photographs. In one picture she wore a black evening dress. She was standing beside a pool, and she was pregnant. I looked up at her. She looked at me, smiling.

"Do you have children?" I asked.

She laughed.

"Do you?"

She shook her head and turned the page. In the next photo she wore hot pants and a T-shirt with the Penn State logo on it—she wasn't pregnant in this one—and stood beside a stack of oil cans, holding a sign that said something in Spanish.

We looked at two more photo albums. Then I said, feeling that the evening needed a conclusion, "I should leave now," and went down the stairs and out on the porch. I told her as we stood together on the porch that it was nice spending the evening with her and thanked her. The cat I'd seen earlier reappeared, weaving itself between our legs.

"What's 'cat' in Spanish?" I asked looking down at it, then back at her.

"El gato," she said, staring into my eyes.

I repeated the words, and she smiled with her eyes still on me.

"I have a friend that might want to meet you," I said, not thinking what I was saying.

"What?"

"My friend, he might want to meet you."

She looked at me quizzically.

"Goodnight," I said.

"*Buenas noches.*"

The bottle of Beefeater was on the counter when I opened the kitchen door. I got ice and Schweppes from the fridge and made a large gin and tonic. The air in the house was dead. I opened the window in the living room and went outside. I pulled a chaise longue close to the edge of the pool, facing it in the direction of the city, and spread out a towel and lay on it. The view from our backyard wasn't as good as the one from Cam's house, but you could see over the evergreens the lights of East Van, and the port area across the inlet. From down by the water came the distant sound of a freight train's horn. There was the smell of charcoal in the night air. I sipped my drink and gazed at the city and thought about Maria. I thought about being alone with her in her room and putting my hand on her breast and kissing her thick lips, and all that stuff—but it didn't seem to work.

The images that came to mind seemed ridiculous, like badly acted scenes in Duchovny's *Red Shoe Diary* or some other Showcase show, and I couldn't imagine performing them; or if I did perform them, feeling any excitement about them.

It was the same whenever I thought of doing anything with Sadie.

I finished the gin and tonic, and went for another.

At about midnight, I headed in and lay on the sofa. The living-room stereo was on and I raised the volume and tuned to a station playing Chilliwack—my dad had liked Chilliwack.

I must have dozed off, because the next thing I knew the music had stopped and a talk show had taken its place. A male caller was asking the show's host, Dr. Dan, if he should feel jealous about his girlfriend working as a "phone-sex artist."

"Well," Dr. Dan said, sounding amused, "I guess that depends on how *man* you are?"

"What do you mean?" the caller said.

"Well, what does your girlfriend talk to these callers about? Have you ever listened in on a call?"

"Yes."

"You have?"

"Yes."

"And what are they like?"

"Some of them are like, you know," the caller said, "…sexual. But a lot of them, it's just like, some guy whose lonely, and they just want to talk to someone."

"Amazing!" Dr. Dan said. "And people actually *pay* for these calls?"

"Yes.

"Can I ask how much?"

"Um, two seventy-five a minute, I think."

"A minute?"

"Um, yeah."

"The world gets stranger every moment. I can see with a real prostitute—there's something physical there—but to pay someone just to talk to you?"

The caller asked again if he should be jealous. But before I could hear the answer I felt an urgent need to urinate.

Getting up, knocking over the glass on the floor, I stumbled to the washroom. The erection I had made it difficult to let go. I leaned forward so that I wouldn't shoot through the space between the seat and the bowl.

When I got back to the living room, the program on the radio had changed. The host of the new show had a deeper and more serious voice than Dr. Dan. Strange dissonant music was playing in the background.

"Tonight on the show we will be talking to a man in the Northwest who identifies himself as a lycanthrope—in other words, though he himself does not like the term, a werewolf. This is Alan Jacobs. Stay tuned."

I turned off the lights and lowered the volume. Lying on the sofa, I waited for sleep.

Cam contacted me that Saturday. He apologized for his "elusive presence." He explained that he'd been seeing this girl who came from a very old and established family in Brazil. He'd met her at Grouse Mountain, where he now worked. That afternoon he was joining her at the beach, and he invited me to come with him. He would drive, he said.

As we drove downtown that afternoon, he told me how pathetic this city was. The women were hideous, and things were better in Latin America. By the time we hit the Lions Gate on-ramp, he was almost shouting. "Fuck! Look at this," he said, pointing to the backed-up traffic. "The place is fucking paralyzed."

I asked him how things were different in Mexico and he dragged phlegm up from his throat and spat out the window. "It's different," he said. "It's just different."

"Livin La Vida Loca," began again on the stereo, the fifth time since he'd picked me up, and Cam raised the volume.

Ahead of us the lanes of traffic quivered in the July heat. A Volkswagen full of high-school girls idled next to us. I gave a whistle.

"What?" Cam asked.

"Nothing," I said, remembering his post-Mexico view of Canadian women: back-packing, Birkenstock-wearing dykes.

"So," Cam said, "tell me more about this little *amorous* adventure."

I'd mentioned earlier my night with the Mexican girl, and Cam had been intrigued.

"Not much to tell," I said. "We just walked around downtown a bit."

"And in her room?"

"Looked at some photographs."

"Photographs!" He sounded exasperated. "Please tell me they were *at least* nude ones."

When I didn't reply, he said, "Mr. Patterson, Mr. Patterson," and shook his head and slapped the top of the steering wheel. "With these women you got to *take them*. That's what *they* expect. It's part of *their* culture. You have to be *macho*."

I laughed nervously.

"I'm *serious*. Don't tell me you're going to do what you did with that girl at university, the one you wrote me about—Sandy or whatever the hell her name was, that blond one you had the hard-on for—sit around, drive her to meet her boyfriends. Un*fucking* believable."

"Do you want to meet her?"

He looked at me. "Me? Why me?"

"You like Spanish women."

"I've got enough trouble with the Brazilian."

"That's the one we're going to meet today?"

"Maybe. She might be there. I'm not sure." He leaned forward and flexed his muscles, grunting.

The middle lane on the bridge now open, the traffic ahead of us thinned.

When we got on the bridge deck, I looked at the city on our left, its slender, glittering glass towers rising above the edge of Stanley Park's green mass. No matter how many times I saw it, it always seemed to promise something.

Just as we got to the middle of the bridge, Cam said something—but with the windows down, the breeze and the swish of passing cars it was impossible to hear.

"What?" I said leaning back, the gust of wind and the sunlight in my eyes.

"…tell you about last night?"

"You had to take the friend to the hospital?"

"Yeah—but it's even crazier than that," he shouted and interrupted the conversation with an eight-second rendition of G N' R's "You're Crazy."

"This girl, the Brazilian, she's crazy. Last night we went to the Cambie for drinks. Halfway through the evening this other girl—this friend of hers, the one I had to take to the hospital—gets all hot and shaky. So we take her to emergency. We're thinking someone's put something in her drink. But the girl, she's O.D.—ing on coke."

He looked searchingly at me.

"But you know what's incredible about this Brazilian girl. I wanted to stay with her friend, to make sure she was alright. But the Brazilian girl, she wanted to go back partying. *Can you believe that?* Your friend almost *dies* and you want to go out again and party!"

"I guess she's *Livin' La Vida Loca,*" I said.

Cam laughed. "Yeah, livin' la vida loca."

I looked over and saw that he was enjoying the thought.

"How about the friend, the one in the hospital?"

"I took her flowers at the hospital and she seemed okay."

"A real Don Quixote," I said.

"But this *cop*—you should've seen this fuckin' chink. He was waiting for me when I came out of the hospital, when I got in the car. He was like, 'Excuse me sir. Have you had anything to drink?' and I said 'No, I just took my friend to the hospital,' and he said 'Come on. You must have had *something* to drink,' and I said, 'No. I've not had anything to drink,' and he said, 'You must have had a drink of your friend's beer,' and I said, 'No' and he said, '*Come on*, buddy, *just* a sip. You must have had *a* sip—' Fuck. I swear. I wanted to smack that guy."

"What happened?"

"The fucker, he took away my license."

"So you don't have it now."

He looked at me and grinned.

In a souvenir store on Denman Street Cam searched for a sun hat. A Filipino store clerk watched from the front. I was afraid he'd be suspicious of me if I didn't do anything, so I studied a revolving rack of postcards. All showed Vancouver as glass towers between violet mountains and white-capped waves.

"So, are you going to meet this girl?"

"The Mexican?" Cam said standing in front of a mirror and trying a sun hat. "Is she hot? A good body? *Que pedazo de tetas?*"

"So you want to meet her?"

He tossed the hat in the bin. "Why are you trying to get me to date these women?" he said trying another sun hat. "Delve in there yourself. Try heterosexuality for a change."

"What do you mean?" I asked.

"Nothing," he said shaking his head and laughing. "Nothing." He adjusted the brim of the tennis hat and grinned at his reflection in the mirror. "I think I like this one."

The clerk at the counter rang in the hat. "Five forty-five," he said.

Cam handed the clerk a ten-dollar bill and said to me, "You should have seen this cop that stopped me. Fuck man, he was *such* a prick. I wanted to smack him right there."

"Why didn't you?"

"Yeah, why didn't I?" he said taking the change from the clerk. "Thanks—do you think if I found out where he goes and start a fight with him when he's off-duty, I'd get into trouble because he's a police officer?"

The conversation continued as we walked through the tree-shaded streets of the West End, toward the beach. First Cam spoke of exacting revenge on the police officer, then about what he should do with the Brazilian girl. As I listened I couldn't tell if Cam liked the girl or disliked her. One minute he said she was out of control and that he had to stop seeing her. The next, that she was very beautiful and came from a strict Catholic family.

"You know one thing that's fucked up? That homestay father. He's a total fucking pervert, I was talking to the Columbian guy—he's also staying at the house—and he said that this homestay father, he buys this girl wine. That when his wife was away, he had the girl upstairs and he made dinner for her and they drank wine together, and then danced."

"What does the girl say?"

"The girl—she's very innocent. She just thinks he's being nice."

Before we reached English Bay, Cam wanted to stop. We sat at the top of a grass slope that overlooked the water. The weather that afternoon was clear. The harbour dotted with sailboats. Freighters in the distance.

Cyclists and rollerbladers glided by on the paved walk below us.

"So…is Damien out yet?"

The question came out of nowhere, and surprised me—it was the first time he'd mentioned Damien.

"I think they're still adjusting his medication," I said.

There was long pause before he said, "He'd probably never be on drugs in the first place if he hadn't broken that window.

"And we know *who* told him to do *that*," he added, insinuatingly, "and then ran around outside to get a better look."

I didn't reply.

"Can I ask you something?" His tone was different.

"Yeah?" I said.

He was looking at the ocean. "Have you ever thought you might just *lose it*?"

"What do you mean?"

"You *know* what I mean."

I swallowed. Tape was stuck to my shoe, and I pulled it off. I gazed back at the distance. I didn't know what he meant—or I didn't want to.

"What? Like Damien?"

He let out a half-laugh. He shook his head and smiled wanly. "No. *Farther* than that."

I studied the sole of my right shoe. A small stone was caught in my tread. I searched the grass, found a twig and dug at the stone, feeling all the while like I was in one of those scenes in a movie where the guy turns to his friend for help and the friend gives his buddy advice, and the advice turns out to be wrong. When I got the stone loose, I dug at another one.

"Sorry, am I scaring you?"

"No. It's fine," I said and threw the twig aside. "I think you should see someone." As I said this I felt like a ham actor reading lines from a TV drama script.

He shook his head.

"Why?'

"Pride, Mr. P., Pride."

I stared back at English Bay and realized, almost with horror, what a beautiful day it was. Clear. Bright.

"Just forget about it," he said.

"How about now? Are you okay now?"

"Now's okay."

I nodded. "So you're not going to blow that cop away?"

I knew that's not what he was talking about, and that I shouldn't be changing the topic—but Cam laughed.

I laughed too, and the mood lightened.

"I would love to waste that chink," he said, and mimicked the sound of a gun firing.

Thinking of the maniac and the parked car and Brad's (or Chad's or whatever his name's) head exploding, I laughed again.

Cam sighed. "I think I'm in love. I think I'm in love," he said.

"With who? The Brazilian?"

He giggled.

The fact that he said this just after his previous announcement frightened me. But I tried not to think about it.

"Let's go," I said.

We both stood up. I dusted off the back of my jeans. *Things will be okay*, I told myself. *Things will be okay.*

The beach was crowded and it took at least five minutes to find a spot. Cigarette butts and wood chips speckled the sand. I cleared away a discarded French fry container and spread out my towel. Cam sat on a log next to me, pulling off his white Nike shirt and exposing his dark, rippled chest.

"Are you going in the water?"

"No," he said glancing up and down the beach. "You go. I'm going to wait here."

Still disturbed by what he had said—or feeling that I should be—I headed into the water. The water was cold. It was cold, and I gasped when a wave hit my groin and my muscles tightened as I dove into those cold waves, the intense sensations pushing all thoughts from my head. I swam metres through the salt water under the surface, and opening my eyes, stared into the dark mud-filled nothingness.

When I surfaced, the skin on my back burned. I wiped hair from my eyes and crouched low in the cold water, the breeze off the ocean suddenly freezing. Two boys, splashing near me, shouted something about a shark.

A metal barge was moored about fifty-feet from shore. It would be used later in the summer for The Symphony of Fire. Closer, there was a small diving platform. A slide was on top, and bathers were sliding down it.

I pushed off and swam out and climbed up the ladder. The dry wooden planks were scorching. As I lay down on them, my back actually felt like it might get burnt. High up in the blue sky a thin streak of cloud lay frozen. I closed my eyes. The ocean breeze was cold on my wet skin. When it paused, the sundry sounds came to my ears, the shrill cries of children and the clanking sound of people rocketing down the slide. I enjoyed the blank feeling of these sensations. I enjoyed the clean, empty feeling they gave me and I lay there another minute. When I sat up and opened my eyes, blotches appeared on my vision. At the raft's edge there was a girl of about fifteen. She sat with her legs in the water. Her face reminded me of my cousin Emily's, but this girl's breasts were larger. But then Emily's breast might be larger too—I hadn't seen her in a year. I guessed I would get to see at Harrison, at the end of summer, if they'd changed. This girl arched her back, adjusting the strap of her turquoise bikini, and I closed my eyes again and tried to recall Maria's face. I saw Cam's face instead. I imagined him standing behind her. Her head fallen against his broad shoulder. His hand sliding down her front. Her breasts in his large hands. Her brown nipples between his fingers. Her mouth half open.

I sat up quickly, and covered my crotch with my left arm.

Cam had left my jeans and T-shirt lying on my towel unattended. I checked to see if my wallet was still in my jeans, and scanned the beach for Cam. When I found him he was standing near the footpath, talking to two guys, and I picked up my things and headed to join them.

One of the guys I suppose was good-looking, with a kind of James-Dean haircut, but he was very short. Cam introduced him as Stephan and said he was from Switzerland. The other guy, Lance, was tall and lanky and from some country I'd never heard of before.

The conversation they were having was about how to pick up women, how to bang women, how to get rid of women after you bang them.

Bored, I said that I was going to go take a piss.

The washroom was cool, and I blinked a number of times as my eyes adjusted to the dimness. The urinal, an old-style one, was a raised step before a tiled wall with a trough at its base. The standing area was gritty with sand I imagined to be soaked with urine, so I stood on the sides of my feet—afraid that I would contract AIDS through some microscopic cuts on my soles.

When I went to the sink to wash my hands, I noticed that the doors to the toilet stalls only went halfway up, and wondered if this was to prevent people from having sex or from doing drugs.

You delve in there yourself. Try heterosexuality for a change.

I washed my hands.

When I came out, Cam had disappeared again, my clothes and towel lying on the grass beside where he and the two men had stood. Thinking perhaps he'd gone to the washroom or to the concession stand, I sat on the log beside the path to wait. A rollerblader passed me with his dog and then a woman with very long hair. The hair moved suddenly and I saw that she wasn't wearing a top.

It took another twenty minutes to figure it out, but Cam had left without me.

Maria looked slightly sunburned. She leaned forward and kissed my left cheek.

"'ola," she said.

"Hola."

We were standing at the corner of Denman and Robson. Maria's white jeans and T-shirt looked purple in the twilight.

"Let's go," I said.

Crowds swarmed past us. One of the drunken teens walking in front of Maria shouted, "She's a skank." He wasn't talking about her, but I wondered if she understood the term.

The light was fading. An uneasiness was in the air. Again I felt that feeling I'd felt that day on Robson Street, the feeling that people were watching us, that someone would come out of nowhere and punch me in the face.

At the bottom of Denman, something was happening. I knew it was a fight from the loud boos and gasps, and saw over the shoulders and between the backs of heads, a blood-covered face; I pushed closer.

But Maria tugged my sleeve. We untangled ourselves from the group and headed toward the beach. Whiffs of marijuana came on the breeze. The dusk sky was rippled with grey and scarlet, the water of English Bay luminous.

I glanced back at Maria and breathed in deeply, making a face. She laughed.

As soon as the fireworks were over, people surged back toward the city. It was too crowded for me to think and I reached for Maria's hand and made my way through them. I'd grabbed the hand so that she wouldn't lose me, but wondered if she thought it meant something, and if it did mean something.

Downtown, we headed north on Granville, jostling through beggars and street protestors, past lines of night-clubbers, street kids with their pet dogs and "Hungry" signs, past sidewalk merchants' velvet-covered tables, turquoise and silver jewellery, past the entrances to sex shops, mannequins in bondage gear in a window, past a busker who coughed and began "Sweet Leaf" on his acoustic, past an arcade, past this man in a brown business suit with padded shoulders who yelled in front of a movie theatre "Just as in the days of Noah... just as in the days of Noah!"

And all the while the smell of marijuana came steadily on the breeze and my hand in Maria's glanced her hip, and for a second I felt connected to the city.

Two goths with a German shepherd sat beside the door of the McDonald's on Smithe. On the way in, I tossed the change I had in my pocket in their turned-up fedora.

A Japanese woman was waiting in the line-up, her arms crossed. She had high black boots and a mask-like face.

Maria was hungry. I got two apple pies.

As we sat and ate, we talked. I asked her how to say a few things in Spanish, and I said them, and she giggled.

She looked at me and asked if I had a girlfriend. I said no. I asked her if she had a boyfriend. She said no.

The house's porch light, shining through the passenger-side window, silhouetted Maria's head. She turned to face me. I didn't say anything. She leaned over and kissed my lips. We kissed again. Then one more time. I enjoyed the feeling of the kisses. We kissed gently three or four more times and we opened our mouths and I put my tongue in her mouth and felt her tongue reaching for mine. I didn't know what to do, so I moved my tongue around and around. After doing this for a while, I got bored and wondered if I could touch her breasts. *With the Spanish women, you've got to take them.* This repeated itself in my head and I imagined recounting the scene to Cam, and felt the need to make it more interesting. But still I was nervous. If she stopped me, I would feel cheap and dirty. I placed my left hand gently against her stomach and moved it gradually toward her breasts, expecting to be stopped. I reached inside the bottom of her T-shirt and again lay my hand against her stomach. The skin was soft, it was hot and smooth. I left my hand there a minute, while I kissed and hugged her. I slid my hand toward her breast—I felt certain that she would stop me. She didn't. I grabbed her breast through the rough lace of her bra and squeezed it three times and pulled back the cup and pinched the nipple. The nipple was large and firm and I flicked it back and forth with my finger and squeezed the breast. I thought this is what she wanted me to do and I felt excited, but not as much as I thought I would. Doing this, I realized that I was forgetting to move my tongue in her mouth. All this was exciting for a few minutes, but then I was again bored. Almost without me even noticing that they were doing it, my fingers began to play with her nipple much as they would a small coin in my pocket or a spring. After another minute, I pulled her bra cup back in place. I got out and went around to the other side and let her out. As she stepped out of the car I felt weird, like it was the first time I was seeing her that evening. The person whom I'd been kissing and whose breast I'd fondled seemed like someone entirely different.

During the midsummer long weekend at the beginning of August, I seemed to be the only person left in Vancouver. Kris was at a real estate convention in Whistler, Alex was at her family's cabin in The Shuswaps, Damien was at home but only wanted to stay indoors and play Nintendo, Sadie was on the Island, and whenever I called Maria the male roommate said she was out.

As for Cam, I'd called his house over the past two weeks and left at least ten messages on his machine. He hadn't returned one of them.

The Police's "Message in a Bottle" was on the poolside radio. I swam six laps, then crouched in the shallow end and held my breath. Everything was silent except for the muffled sound of the music and the gurgling of the pool's filtration system. Still under, I remembered Paul Ramsey, my friend's older brother, doing this. He had seen some documentary about Polynesian skin divers—the ones who go six or seven minutes without air—and began to practice himself. His parents figured that was what he had been doing when it happened—at least, that's what they told people. No one really knows though, because no one else was at home. They returned from Hawaii and the body was floating in the pool.

My throat and lungs now burned. I held my breath longer and thought of what it would be like if I lost consciousness—passed out, died. I could imagine Damien and Cam and Alex standing around and looking at my casket. But what I couldn't imagine was where it would be. When my parents died they were cremated, I remember being told that, and told that we were going to do something with the ashes—but I can't remember if we ever did. And my grandparents, they both had small graveside services, but that was because they'd requested them.

If I died, what would Kris do? Cremate me? Bury me?

I shot up to the surface.

Taking deep breaths, I got out, towelled myself dry, then lay on one of the green chaises. Tea Party's "Temptation" had come on. I clicked off the radio and settled back in the chaise. There was a light breeze. The faint drone of a neighbour's mower and sunlight filtering through the hemlocks made me drowsy. As I lay there, struggling not to drift off, more images of neighbours' deaths flickered through my memory: the son of Dr. Haroldson, the psychiatrist, who hanged himself from the chandelier in the front hall; the Korean family that after a whole summer day of the RCMP going in and out of their silent Tudor-style house was never seen again; the renter in the house next door who was found asphyxiated during Expo 86—all these things had happened in the summer.

I went inside.

When it started to get dark, I put on a pair of chinos and T-shirt and went down to Burger King for dinner. After, I rented *Magic* and *Sleep Away Camp II*.

4

"So—how do you know this place?"

"What?"

"The place, the Cave."

"Everyone knows about it," she said. She turned up the volume on the car stereo. "I love this song."

"Everyone?"

"Yeah," she said. "Listen."

The lyrics were about penetration and violation, and I didn't think I recognized the song. But when the chorus began I remembered Alex playing the song for me in her room, telling me that it was Nine Inch Nail's "Closer."

"This place we're going, it's not like that apartment on Lonsdale?"

Alex looked at me, her eyes wide. "How do *you* know about that place?"

"Everyone knows about it," I said trying to imitate her insouciant tone.

"No—seriously—how do you know?"

"Some girls at your party, they were talking."

"What did they say?"

"Don't you have this CD?"

"Tell me," she said, turning off the radio. "What did they say?"

"Nothing. Just that some guy—"

"They didn't say anything about me?"

"No. Why? Do you go there?"

"You *promise* they didn't say anything about me."

"Yes—why? Have you been there?"

"Shhh. I want to hear this," Alex said and turned back on the radio.

"Don't you have the CD?"

"Yeah. But it's better on the radio."

"Why? How?"

"I don't know. It's like you're connected to all those people. The people you know are listening to it."

"Sure," I said, but then thought about it and realized it made sense.

The house we were going to that night was owned by a Korean family, but they didn't live there, they lived in Korea, and no one had ever seen the son who supposedly took care of the house for them.

When we got there it was around nine. Kids had spilled out on the lawn and were staggering and falling in the grey twilight. Two boys in navy and maroon hoodies stood at the top of the driveway hackysacking, while a third boy lay on the grass beside them.

"Shouldn't we turn him over?" I heard one boy say as I passed. "Isn't that how Pat died?"

The front door was open and we shouldered our way through the group standing there and went up the stairs and into the kitchen. More high-school kids circled the kitchen island. A bottle of shaken-up Coke stood on it, and they were having some type of argument about alcohol.

"Isn't, like, Crystal's mother supposed to get it?"

"Didn't you hear what I said, Roach? She failed some socials test. Now her mother's angry at her."

The girl with the tank top nodded. She stuck out her tongue, and pulling it back, banged her teeth with the metal stud.

"Hey, isn't he old enough to go?" I heard one of the boys say.

I wasn't sure if he was referring to me, but I followed Alex down the hallway on the right. In the bedroom at the end two girls, maybe fifteen or sixteen, sat cross legged on the floor.

"Bead!" Alex said to the girl on the left. "Hey—do you know who's got some pot?"

"Um—" Between them on the floor was a boy, and they appeared to be minding him. "I think Reese has some."

"Where is he?"

The boy was young, maybe eleven or twelve, and he was naked except for a green tartan kilt. He rolled to the left, and then to the right, and flailed his arm above his head, trying to reach the overturned bottle of Flintstone multi-vitamins behind him. When he rolled to the left the kilt came up, and I saw that he wasn't wearing any underwear. The penis, small, pale and limp, stuck to the side of his scrotum, and there was no pubic hair.

"Josh! Josh!" the girl on the right said. She pulled down on the kilt. But the boy's body was lying on the material, and she couldn't get it down far enough to cover him. "Josh, cover up! We can see your *pee pee*."

"Is Garth here?"

"Nope."

"Yeah he is," the girl on the right said.

"Garth's not here."

The boy got hold of the vitamin bottle. He shook it like a rattle.

"He's in Surrey. I talked to him last night."

"I think he's back."

"No. He's not."

"Are you sure?"

"Positive."

Josh held the bottle high over his upturned face. He poured out a bunch of Flintstones and chomped on them with his mouth open.

"I don't think Josh has any," Alex said.

"Are you sure?"

"Positive."

"*Oh*, my *God*! Bead. *Bead*—"

"Check down stairs. I think—"

"Bead. Look—Josh's eaten the vitamins. He's eating the vitamins."

The boy's face was glazed with saliva and coloured bits of half-chewed Flintstones.

"Anyway—"

"Did you *hear* me?"

"Well don't spaz about it."

"He could die."

"Trish, you can't die from Flintstones."

"Yeah! You can! My cousin ate them, and he had to have his stomach pumped."

In the kitchen I told Alex, "I'm going to stay here."

"Are you okay?" she asked.

"Yeah. Why?"

"You look sad."

I shrugged. "I'm fine." I noticed a sofa through the doorway behind Alex and pointed. "I'm going to wait in there."

"Are you sure?"

"Uh huh."

Sitting on the sofa, I pulled out the Smirnoff I'd brought and unscrewed the top and took a swig. It wasn't cold enough and I sputtered. I took another one. I put the bottle back in my pocket and looked around the room. It was supposed to be some kind of family room. But the walls were decorated with faded pages cut from a porno magazine, and on the far wall I thought I saw one of Kris's calendars. I couldn't imagine any Korean family living here. The stereo in the corner was on and the first notes of "Born on the Bayou" wobbled out of the speakers. The fat boy on the couch adjacent to mine stared psychotically at the rug. He sipped a Super Big Gulp, and then swore under his breath. Two other boys were playing *Super Mario* on an old Nintendo. All three of them were dressed in baggy plaid shirts, and I felt like I was in some sort of grunge video or a scene from the movie *Kids*.

Another boy entered the room. He also wore a plaid shirt and held up a Handycam to his face. He turned down the stereo and approached the fat kid, videotaping him. "Hey Chris," he said. "Say something really sick."

"Fuck you, Cory."

"Come on. You can do better than that. Just one thing."

"I fucked your grandmother last night."

"That's better. Did it feel good?"

"Yeah."

"As good as your mother?"

The fat kid kicked out at the boy with the Handycam, but that boy had jumped back, keeping the Handycam fixed on the fat boy's face.

I had the bottle out again and I took another sip. It was getting easier. I needed to use the toilet.

In the washroom, I was afraid to touch anything. I pulled down my sleeve and handled everything through it. I remembered Vincent, Damien's psych-ward roommate, and worried that I was turning into him.

When I got back to the family room, Josh the boy from the bedroom was there. He was in the middle of the room and was doing an awkward sort of dance, holding the hem of his kilt with both hands and swaying it back and forth. After doing this for maybe a minute, he lay with his face on the floor and raised his ass high in the air. He wiggled it back and forth, and the kilt fell over his back. Behind him, the two boys now watched some kind of home movie on TV.

"Watch this," one of them said. On the screen someone vomited into a toilet bowel.

"Gross," the other said.

"Hi. What's your name?" a girl said, sitting down beside me. She was the one from the kitchen, the one in the scarelet tank top and spiky hair who couldn't understand why the other girl's mother wouldn't run liquor for them.

For some reason I was reluctant to give her my real name, and said, "Paul. And yours?"

"Roach."

"Roach?" I said, certain that I'd misheard.

"Yeah, Roach. My parents call me Rachel, but don't call me that. I *hate* that name."

For a minute, neither one of us said anything.

In the middle of the room, the fat kid had got off the sofa and stood over Josh. He'd found a cardboard tube somewhere, like the ones that posters come in, and began to spank Josh's bare ass with it.

"Who did you come with?"

"Alex Murphy," I said.

The girl looked up as if thinking about it. Again she stuck out her tongue and was tapping her teeth with the piercing.

"She has short blonde hair," I said.

The fat kid had stopped spanking Josh with the tube, and instead tried to push it into Josh's ass.

Josh, his face still on the floor, feigned an expression of pleasure, and he wiggled his ass back and forth as if trying to assist the fat kid.

My little cock can go where big cocks can't.

"I don't think I know her," the girl said. "Listen, is it true you're nineteen?"

"Uh. Yeah," I said, and waited for her to ask me to get them alcohol.

"Isn't that illegal?"

"What?"

"That girl and you—you know."

"What do you mean?"

For a half-minute, the girl didn't respond, then jumping up, said, very emphatically, like she was acting some role, "Don't worry. Your secret's *Safe. With. Me.*"

Before I could say anything, she'd skipped back into the kitchen.

The fat boy had given up and gone back to the couch and the Slurpee. One of the boys who'd been watching the TV now picked up the cardboard tube. He poked Josh's bum with it. But as he did this, Josh reached around and grabbed it. He yanked it from the boy's hand. The boy stepped back as Josh jumped up. Josh hit the boy surprisingly hard on the side of the head with the tube. The boy ran into the kitchen, Josh chasing him

The feeling the vodka had given me was gone. When I got the bottle out again it was half empty.

Give it time.

Alex didn't want to go home. She lay in the backseat of the car and insisted I take her somewhere.

"Where do you want to go?" I asked.

"I don't care. Anywhere."

Horseshoe Bay seemed as good as anywhere.

An almost full moon shone down as we drove the highway, some DJ on one of the stations playing Harvey Danger's "Flagpole Sitta" over and over again. As always, I had the windows down.

When we got back from Horseshoe Bay, I headed to take Alex home, but she didn't want to go there.

"Is your dad home?" I finally asked.

She didn't answer, but after a pause said, "He wants to meet you."

At my house I lay on my bed while Alex paced my room.

There were posters on the wall from the days when my grandparents operated a drive-in in northern BC, and Alex paused for a long time in front of the one for *Ice Man.*

"NO rhyme, no reason, just death," she said, reading the caption.

"The poster's from my grandparents' movie theatre," I said. "My grandparents, they used to own a drive-in movie theatre—in the seventies. *Ice Man* was one of the movies."

Alex went to the bookshelf and looked at the titles.

"Wow, have you read all of these?"

"Yeah. Most of them."

She pulled out *Animal Farm*, a hardcover I'd inherited when our neighbour, who was some kind of book collector, died.

"We had to read this one in school," she said. "It was so boring."

"You didn't like it?"

"I only read half of it. Then—I think I lost it."

She pushed it back.

"What's this one about?" she asked, pulling out a copy of *Sons and Lovers*

"Um… it's about this guy with this really domineering mother and—"

"There's this one book," she said, replacing *Sons and Lovers*, "Farid told me it has all this really dirty—"

"There's a lot of books like that."

"But this one's really famous."

"*Ulysses?*"

"It was something about cancer."

"*Tropic of Cancer?*"

"Maybe."

"You can get it at the library."

"Doesn't it have all this sex and stuff?"

"Yeah. But you can still get it at the library."

"Why are you reading this?" she asked, looking alarmed. She'd pulled out Durkheim's *Suicide*, an edition with a blank red cover with "suicide" written across it in bold white letters.

"What?" I laughed, thinking that she probably thought it was some kind of how-to guide, with diagrams on how to tie nooses and put them over your neck. "It's just a study on suicide. I had to read it for a Sociology class."

"*Still*—it looks *really* weird," she said, pushing it back on the shelf.

I began to think about the book and said, "It says there's four social reasons why people kill them themselves. If they don't connect with the people around them… if they—"

"You like books?"

"Sometimes. Do you?"

"No, not really," she said.

She turned around and walked toward me. There was a strange expression on her face.

"Here, let's do something."

She got down on her knees in front of me. She looked up at me. She unbuttoned my jeans and tried to yank them down.

"Get up."

I had my hands on the bed behind me and I lifted my butt up. She pulled down my jeans, then my boxer shorts— it happened so fast I didn't have time to feel embarrassed.

"This would be better if I had the stud," she said.

"What—what are you doing?"

She didn't seem to hear me.

"What are you doing?"

After another moment—my penis still flaccid—she stopped.

"What? Don't you want me to do this?"

"I don't know."

Still on her knees, my penis still in her hand, she studied me.

She stood up, wiped her lips on her sleeve and sat beside me on the bed.

"Why? Don't you like me doing that?"

"I don't know."

Another pause.

"You're not gay are you?"

"No."

She smiled, looked away, then back "But you don't like me doing that?"

"So, how's their marriage?" Kris asked. We had been out looking at condos that morning and were now having brunch at Earl's. Somehow the subject of Alex had come up.

"Who? Alex's parents?"

I'd made the mistake of mentioning Alex's father's absences, and Kris had become fixated on the state of their marriage. Kris nodded.

"Is *that* important?"

"It is, if it's falling apart," she said casually.

I felt a dropping feeling in my stomach.

She signalled the waiter to bring more coffee. "It never hurts to know when people are looking for new houses."

"Don't you mean a *home*?" I said, referencing her advertising slogan: *When a house is a home.*

Either she didn't get the dig, or chose to ignore it.

The waiter came with our main order. Kris's eyes stayed on him as he set her eggs Benedict in front of her. He was maybe two years younger than me, but was muscular and had a neatly chiselled haircut. After he left she said, "Is he sleeping with her?"

I thought she was talking about the waiter, then remembered the conversation was about Alex's parents.

"What do you mean?"

"Do they still *sleep* in the *same room*?"

"Should I hide in their closet?" I said, glancing at my bacon. Kris didn't respond, and when I looked up she was glaring.

"*Don't* be sarcastic with me," she hissed. She tried her eggs, and dropped her fork loudly on the plate. "Every time I come here I have to go through the same shit," she said, as if to herself. She looked toward the serving station. "If they're going to get divorced then the house might go on the market," she said, trying to catch the server's eye. "Or they might be looking for separate apartments and townhouses. It never *hurts* to know these things—for heaven's sake Trace. Fuck! *Grow up*! Do you think you're the only one *suffering* here? Act like—"

"Is everything alright?" the waiter asked.

"Oh, it's delicious," Kris said. "But."

"Is something the matter?"

"Well—" She pointed at the eggs Benedict and began to hem and haw, as if she were too polite to complain.

"I'll talk to the kitchen."

As he took back the order, Kris's eyes didn't lose him.

"You know they're going to spit on it," I said.

"Maybe at the places *you* go to."

The server was at the open kitchen, talking to a person who looked like an older version of himself in a chef's hat. I remembered what Sadie'd told me about working here—in order to talk to the cooks the servers had to ask permission.

The chef did not look happy, and I could picture him taking people's orders into the back and doing something disgusting to them. I laughed.

"I'm glad *you're* in such a good mood," Kris said.

As we were leaving Earl's, a man called out, "Here's my number-one competitor." Michael Daniels rose from one of the tables on the patio. He held out his hand, then seemed to change his mind, and hugged Kris instead. He was in his late forties and had what I guess people called rugged handsomeness.

"How are you?"

"Good," Kris answered, sounding tense.

"Out for lunch?"

"That's a nice way of putting it," she said under her breath.

"And is this?" He glanced back at Kris.

"Yes," she said, "this is Jack's son."

"Excellent," he said. "I didn't know your father as a young man. But, boy, is there a resemblance."

Michael began to talk to Kris about the real estate market; I enjoyed watching her squirm. She envied Michael and always claimed that it was from her that he had stolen his famous slogan, *When you're not just buying a house, but a Home.*

The answering machine was flashing. I pressed play. The message from Cam asked me to call him. I dialled the number, thinking that it was futile. But Cam answered.

"Trace—" he shouted.

"Hi. You called?"

"Yeah. How's it going?" he said, sounding like he was pretending to be relaxed.

"Not bad. I was just out to lunch. How about you?"

"Not bad, not bad. How are you?"

I was still annoyed by how he'd deserted me at the beach. But his jovial tone made me decide to drop the issue. "Pretty good," I said.

There was long pause before he spoke again. "Do you know where I can get coke from?"

"What?"

"Do you know where I can get coke from?" he said more slowly.

"I assume you don't mean the kind that comes in a bright red bottle."

"Don't be fucking stupid."

I thought about it. I could probably get it off a girl I knew at university, but I didn't want to get involved. "I don't think so."

"Come on!" said Cam. "You must know someone. How about that girl that liked you last year?"

"Tiffany? I haven't talked to her in, like, a long time."

"Can't you call her?"

"She's—not here. She's in Montreal or Toronto, I think."

"So you don't know anyone?"

"I don't know anyone."

There was a pause, and I sat in the desk chair.

"The girl, the Brazilian, she's having this party and her friends like to do a bit but they don't know anyone they can trust—what's the fucking problem?"

"Is there one?"

A long exasperated sigh came over the line. When he spoke again though, he was amicable. "Anyway, things are good?"

"Can't complain. You sure you're alright?"

"Great," he said.

"So—what happened at the beach?"

"Oh yeah. Sorry. The Brazilian girl came. Her friends were going to this movie so we had to go. Sorr—how about the guy you used to hang out with in Surrey?"

Cam stopped at the house at about ten the next night. I could tell when he came in the door that he was upset about something.

As we played Nine-ball on the pool table in the basement, he told me that he was now certain that the Brazilian girl's homestay father was going to try to fuck her, that "the bastard" was going to use drugs to do it.

"Why don't you fuck him up?" I said as a joke.

Cam looked at me seriously: "You mean beat him up in front of the Brazilian girl?"

"You boys still up?" Kris said, coming into the room. I guess with the loudness of Cam's voice and the Oasis we were listening to, I hadn't heard her come home. She was wearing a blue kimono and carried a large glass of white wine.

"Why? Why don't you think it's a good idea?" Cam said, seemingly oblivious to my aunt's presence.

"Hello, Cameron," she said.

"Oh—sorry Mrs. Patterson." He really mustn't have noticed her, because he was startled.

Kris brushed off a chair and sat down in it. "That's okay. How are you?'

"Good," he said—his tone for the first time that evening sounding amiable.

"I suppose I should apologize for my attire." She took from the pocket of the housecoat a fresh package of Matinée and began to peal the plastic wrapper off. "But I didn't think Trace had company."

"Should I leave?" he said and glanced from her to me.

"No, no, it's fine," she said. "It's actually nice to have company. Steve went to bed. You don't mind if I smoke, do you?"

Neither Cam nor I answered the question.

I'd finished racking the balls and said, "It's your turn."

"So Cameron, Trace tells me that you've been travelling all over the world."

"Um, no, just Mexico," Cam said and leaned down. He took the shot and scratched. "Fuck!" he said, then looking embarrassed, turned to Kris. "Sorry Mrs. Patterson."

103

"Oh, don't worry about it. You can't be married to four different men and not hear a bit of swearing," she said as if it were a joke.

"Try again," I said to Cam.

Cameron rolled the cue ball behind the line. His second attempt was successful, the diamond of balls shattering, and the two ball falling in the right centre pocket. He attempted to put the one ball in the left corner pocket; but the angle was wrong, and the ball hit the bumper left of the pocket and rolled to a stop in the centre of the table.

"Where in Mexico did you go?"

"This small resort town south of Mexico City, Cuernavaca. I don't know if you heard of it."

I approached the table and tried for the one ball.

"I remember when I used to go cruising, and we went to Acapulco and Puerto Vallarta. Those places were so beautiful."

"Okay. Your turn." I'd left the two ball snookered behind the five.

"Yeah. I hear those places are nice."

Cam tried to bank the ball off the end bumper to hit the two, but missed.

I picked up the cue ball and placed it behind the three ball, tried with a combo shot to sink the nine.

"So did you meet any attractive señoritas?" Kris asked.

I looked to Cam's face for the reaction.

A wan smile. "No, not really" he said.

"Oh, I can't believe that," Kris said her eyes glued on Cam. "You are a very handsome young man. Women *must* adore you."

"Your shot," I said.

"I guess," Cam said to Kris.

"Cam, your shot."

We played one more game. Then I said I wasn't feeling well. I thought I was going to throw up. Cam started to leave, but Kris was angry; I was being rude, she said. She stood up to stop Cam from leaving, then stumbled and fell.

When Cameron and I helped her to her feet, she looked as if she were about to cry.

Cam had gone home, and I was taking off my boxers when Kris burst into the room.

"What—"

She wasn't wearing anything except blue panties. The outline of her maxi pad visible between her thighs.

"How do you turn this stupid thing off?" She twisted one dial of my stereo, then another.

"Here. Don't touch it," I said, reaching for the volume.

"Don't shout."

"I'm not."

"Turn if *off*!"

"I am."

"Don't shout at me—Is it off?"

"What does it sound like?"

She slapped me.

"What the hell?" I said finally.

"Don't ever talk to me like that."

"Why'd you hit me?"

She shoved a note pad in my face. The pad she was holding was one of the ones I'd doodled on: her face marred by two Frankenstein-like scars, a unicorn horn protruding from her forehead.

"Explain."

My cheek still smarted from the slap.

"Yeah. Not very smart. I'm meeting a client tomorrow morning. Do you have any idea what *shit* would have happened if I hadn't looked at this before I put it in my case? If I got there and handed him one?"

I shrugged.

"I suppose you and your retard friend did this when you were drinking."

"Cam?"

"No."

"Damien? He's not retarded."

"You're the retarded one. He's just nuts—And *this*!" She was holding up a crunched ball of paper. "This is the property assessment, and it looks like you blew your nose in it."

I remembered that piece of paper.

"Real mature, Trace. Real fucking mature."

2:04 A.M.

"So you've worked at Section 4?"

"I was a technician there."

"What did you see when you were at Section 4? We've had other callers who worked at Section 4 and they reported that the government was holding aliens there."

There was a burst of noise, like the caller had dropped the phone.

"Hello?" Alan Jacob said. "Are you still with us?"

"I can't talk any longer," the caller said, panicking. "They'll triangulate my position any moment now."

"Hold on. Hold on. Our listeners need to know this. Other people who worked at Section 4 said that these—these aliens—are not aliens."

"They are not aliens as we think of as aliens," gasped the caller. "They—oh my god!—they are not from outer space. They are from another dimension. They are spiritual entities."

"And is it true they have now taken control of some high ranking members of the C.I.A. and—"

"Oh god! God! No." A click.

"Hello. Caller, you still there?"

Pause.

"Okay—"

Pause.

"We've lost him."

I didn't hear from Cam for another week. By the time he called that Friday night I'd already made plans to go drinking with Damien, though I hesitated telling Cam because he got weird when I hung out with Damien. Things had gotten worse with the Brazilian and he really wanted to do something. After he repeated this a fifth time, I told him what I was doing. When he didn't say anything, I suggested he join us, and to my surprise, he accepted.

A pale green sky spread high above the bridge's towers. My bangs flapped in the ocean breeze. "Tell me a story, Mr. Patterson," Cam said as we dropped back down into the causeway. We were in his dad's new convertible and the top was down. "What's been going on?"

I'd had another run-in with Kris as I was leaving that night, and it disturbed me more than I'd realized.

"Come on! Tell me something."

Headlights of the cars coming at us smeared into lines with the taillights ahead. I pictured a pair crossing the median. Imagined the sensations of the crash.

"*Tell* me something," Cam shouted.

"Did you know about Trent Peaks?" I said, suddenly remembering gossip from one of Alex's party.

Cam shook his head.

"You didn't hear about him?"

"No."

"He got that scholarship to SFU to play basketball," I said, "you know that, right?"

Cam nodded.

"Well, he didn't go right away. His parents said that he could take the year off, relax a bit. So he went up to Whistler—the family I think owns some kind of chalet up there. And Trent goes up and, you know, just hangs around, snowboarding and stuff. And after about a month or so his parents get a call from this girl he's living with up there. And she says, he's doing *way* too many drugs and—"

But I had to stop. Cam was laughing too much; and I started to laugh, too.

When I thought I could continue I tried to finish the story, but had to wait another minute or so before the laughter subsided enough that I could speak: "And when his parents—*His Parents*—they went to get him, he. He's—*totally* gone. They brought him home and. And he lay on the floor in his room all day, curled up. In a little ball and crying."

After we stopped laughing, Cam and I were pretty much silent. I wondered how he and Damien were going to react to each other. In high school they were better friends with each other than either one had been with me. But near the end of Grade 12, there was a falling out. At first I thought this was because of the car accident; but later I suspected that the accident was an excuse, that the real reason Cam broke off his friendship with Damien was that he saw too much of himself in Damien and that, for him, Damien's time in the hospital was a premonition.

Damien sat alone in one of the booths at the bar, smoking a cigarette. A half-empty pitcher of brown ale stood in the centre of the table, next to an empty schooner, a pack of Dunhill, and the Zippo lighter.

Cam nodded in greeting and slid into the booth beside him.

The bar's house band was a CCR cover band, and we listened to the first two verses of "Bad Moon Rising" before Cam mentioned Mike Tyson "chomping" on Evander Holyfield's ear—he and Damien exploded in conversation. They cut each other off in mid-sentence and their eyes flashed with the same intensity they'd had in high school, a dark, relentless intensity that had frightened others. But side by side across the table, their faces becoming more animated and their voices rising in volume, it was obvious how much they'd changed. They were no longer the two guys who had slightly long hair, who wore black Metallica and G N' R t-shirts, who wore jean jackets with torn-off sleeves and Led Zeppelin written on the back in Jiffy markers. Damien had gained weight and sported a shaggy beard and his long hair was greasy. Cam, in contrast, was clean-shaven and neat and the new leather jacket he wore made him look like one of the guys he and Damien used to mock in high school for trying too hard to get women.

A waitress asked if anyone would like to order. She was in her early twenties, and had dyed black hair and a ring in her top lip. Cam said that he was fine. Damien and I agreed to share a pitcher of Okanagan Lager.

Damien and Cam resumed talking about Mike Tyson, how the guy was an animal and how he raped that woman; then talked about Guns N' Roses, Cam saying that they had cleaned up now and were back in the studio to record a new album, and Damien saying that he'd heard that Slash was still using.

And as they said these things I didn't try to join the conversation. I was content that they were finally talking.

I worked my way through the pitcher and glanced every now and then around the bar. In the corner there was a girl who looked a bit like Alex. Then I thought of Maria. Since the night in the car I hadn't spoken to her once. I'd called her house a number of times, but got either Fernando, who always said that she was out, or the family's answering machine: "*The Janzens are in Europe. Call back in September.*"

The band took a break. To my ears numb from the ten-minute rendition of "Suzie Q," the clanking of glasses and the loud, slurred voices seemed almost quiet.

But then "Livin La Vida Loca" exploded from the jukebox.

Cam, excited, told Damien that this was "the most fucking brilliant song ever written."

Damien's response: "Fuckin' piece of shit."

After that, Cam's mood changed. Morose, he slouched in the seat, stared at the table, almost glaring.

Damien ordered another pitcher.

Damien laughed.

After two or three minutes of tense silence, Cam stood up. He was going to leave, he announced. He suspected that the Brazilian was at the Avalon and asked if I was coming.

I looked at him. I picked up the coaster and tapped it on the table. I didn't want him to feel deserted. But I thought of my last time at the Avalon, and I didn't want to go back there.

"I'll stay," I said.

He stalked off. By the door he almost ran over the waitress who cowered against the wall to avoid him.

"Wooo," said Damien. He took a deep drag of his cigarette and exhaled, "That guy's *way* too intense."

"Why?"

"You saw him."

Damien set down his cigarette. He leaned on both hands and stared intensely at the table, like he was going to kill it.

I laughed.

Damien raised his cigarette and added, "You'd think he was going through a mid-life crisis or something. He's only, like, what? Twenty?"

When I stopped laughing I felt I should say something in Cam's defence. "I think he's having some problems with his girlfriend, or something."

"No. Fucking. Shit. No woman's going to like that. Women want someone to make them relax, not freak them out."

The girl who resembled Alex reached over the table. As she sat down, she pulled up the back of her jeans and slid the strap of her tank top up on her shoulder. Both gestures reminded me of Alex's, and the girl's short blond hair was identical.

"Is your aunt back yet?"

"From where?"

"From that trip she was on?"

"To the States?"

Damien nodded.

"She's back, but left again."

"Where?"

"I don't know. Somewhere. Vancouver Island."

The girl got out of her chair and was walking toward me.

"Why's she over there?"

"I don't know." I said, looking back at Damien. "I guess some real estate deal, something. She—"

"Trace!"

It *was* Alex.

"Hi."

"What are you doing here?"

"Um, not much. Just drinking."

"Didn't you see me sitting over there?"

"Um. Yeah."

She turned to Damien. "Hi. I'm Alex. I'm Trace's friend." She held her hand out, but Damien only gave a shrug and filled his schooner with beer.

She turned back to me. "Why didn't you come over and say 'Hi?'"

"I don't know. I wasn't sure it was you."

"Are you serious?"

"You were with that guy."

"Leroy? He's just a friend. He's got this band. They're really cool."

I nodded, still feeling strange that she'd called me her friend. "How did you get in here?"

"With this—" She held out a laminated card. It was a driver's license that belonged to a blonde girl named Kirsten McCloy who looked nothing like Alex. "Diane got it for me. She got it from this woman at work. She said it was better to have my own I.D. than to trust, like, older guys who would get me drunk. Take advantage of me."

"Like me?" Damien said, and tried to laugh.

Alex gave him a sarcastic grin. "Your friend's so negative," she said, slapping me on the shoulder while still looking at Damien.

One of the musicians strummed a chord on his Telecaster.

"Reality's negative," Damien mumbled.

The drummer smacked the sticks together four times, and the band started a wobbly version of "Ramble Tamble."

"Anyway, I should get back," Alex shouted. "Why don't you come and join us?"

"Maybe."

When she left, Damien asked where I knew her from.

"I met her at the library, in Edgemont. She's one of the pages."

"And she just started talking to you?"

"Pretty much," I said, not wanting to tell him that she had caught me looking at *The Joy of Sex* and had said that everyone looked like hippies in the book.

"She's not bad looking," Damien said.

I shrugged, pretending I hadn't noticed.

Damien finished the beer, then said, "Do you think she'd give me a blow job?"

At closing time, Alex said they were headed downtown to go clubbing—she asked if we would like to join them. Damien didn't have a car, so I said, "Sure." Damien said he wasn't coming, but when we got out to the parking lot, he climbed in the back seat of the Buick with me.

When we closed the doors, the guy with Alex leaned over the seat and told us his name was Leroy.

I said, "Hi."

Damien ignored him.

We were silent for the first part of the drive. When I asked Leroy about his band, he said he didn't have one. I wanted to ask Alex why she'd said he did, then decided I didn't care. Leroy told Alex that Dead Corpse was playing that Saturday at Seylynn Hall. She said that she had to go shopping in the States with her mother and Leroy said he hated the States. He said that they'd killed more people than Hitler and Stalin combined, and that they had actually already conquered the world, and had set up puppet states like Iraq, so that people would be afraid, and think they needed the States. The book in which he had read this was written by a guy who'd later been killed by the CIA.

Damien made faces behind his back, and I looked out the window so that I wouldn't laugh. But when Damien started chanting "USA! USA!" I got nervous.

Neither Alex nor Leroy said anything, and Damien finally stopped.

"Do you ever listen to Alan Jacob's show," I asked, thinking that was where Leroy'd heard about the conspiracy plot.

"Don't listen to the show," Leroy said, growing very serious. He leaned over the seat. "They put subliminal messages in it. If, like, you listen to twenty hours, then the US government will control you."

"He works for the government?" I said.

"He works for the government."

The car again fell silent. We crossed over the Georgia viaduct and the words "Cobalt Motor Hotel," printed in faded white letters on a brick wall, made me again feel I was in a movie—Paul Hackett in *After Hours,* the preppy who finds himself going "downtown."

The nightclub to which we were headed was called The Rage and we parked beneath the SkyTrain tracks, next to the old Expo grounds.

"Make sure everything is out of sight," Leroy said as we got out.

"Is it dangerous?" Alex asked.

"No, as long as they don't see anything."

Three cars ahead of us a Datsun's passenger-side window was missing, shattered glass glittering on the sidewalk beside it.

"Do you really think my car's okay there?" Alex asked.

"Thieves only break in if they see something they want."

We walked along the chain-link fence. Beyond it the old Expo site was now a wasteland of cracked hardtop.

"Remember Expo 86?" I asked, looking at rusted pipe sticking up out of the ground, recalling the brightly coloured pavilions and arcades and the giant ballroom in the kid zone.

"I can't really remember it," Alex said.

"It was so cool!" said Leroy.

"You know what was so cool?" I said. "Those, like, UFO water parks."

"Oh yeah!" Damien said.

"Oh, I kind of remember that," Alex said.

On the ride home from the club, Damien was completely obnoxious. He swore at Alex and Leroy in the front and accused the doorman at the club of molesting him.

"The guy was a faggot," Damien said.

"How do you know?"

"He touched me," Damien said, looking for something in the pockets of his raincoat.

"He touched all of us."

"That's what I mean," said Damien.

"That's what his job is," Leroy said.

"He was frisking us," Alex said.

"The guy wasn't *frisking* us," Damien said derisively. "The guy was a fucking pervert. He touched my dick I tell you. "

"He did not."

"Yeah, he did. I swear. When he checked my leg, he brushed my fucking dick."

Leroy and I had smoked a joint outside the club and even though I knew Damien was being a complete idiot, I couldn't help cracking up when he said these things.

"Here," Damien said, tapping me on the shoulder. "Do you have my smokes?"

I checked my pocket for the tenth time. "No, I don't have them," I said.

"Fuck! I don't believe it. Not only did he touch my dick. He stole my fucking smokes too."

"Can't you find them?"

"No. I remember I put them in my pocket and now they're not there."

"I'm sure you'll find them."

"I pay seven bucks cover for what? For some fucking faggot to steal my smokes? I pay seven fucking bucks to have my smokes stolen."

"Are you sure they're not in your pocket," Alex offered.

"No, I checked," Damien said, checking the coat's pockets another time. "I don't fucking believe it. I pay seven bucks to have my smokes stolen."

"Well, it wasn't healthy for you, anyway," Alex said.

"Fuck you," Damien said. "You're not healthy for me."

"Do you want me to stop driving?" Alex said suddenly sounding more serious than I'd ever heard her sound before.

"No keep driving, keep driving." Damien said.

"Where are we going, anyway?"

"Someplace we can get beer," Damien said.

"Boston Pizza's still open. They have beer."

"Do you want to go to Boston Pizza?" Alex asked.

No one replied. As we drove through downtown Vancouver, Damien started going on again about how he'd paid seven dollars to have his smokes stolen by a fag. I joked that a fag had stolen his fags, but no one seemed to hear me. When we got into Stanley Park we grew silent. We noticed that something was different. It was darker than usual.

The truck was on the opposite side of the road. Its front end pointed across the lane, its back pressed against the pole that supported the lane-change signals, the pole bent in half. Beneath the engine the flame flickered on the puddle of liquid.

"Is everyone alright?" Alex yelled.

Glass crunched under our feet.

"Help me." The man's voice sounded very small.

"Where are you?"

"Here."

The windshield was missing. We got up to the dark cab. A large man lay on the driver's side. The seat had collapsed backwards and the man didn't move.

"Okay," Alex shouted. "Stay calm."

Damien and I tried the driver's door. It was jammed. I went around to the other side and tried that door, but it didn't move either.

"Fuck! It's going to blow," Leroy shouted.

The wavering glow on the pavement grew brighter—I stepped back.

"Has anyone called 911?"

Stopped in the middle lane was a southbound SUV, the front passenger side window down. Someone had shouted the question from the darkness inside.

"No," Leroy shouted back.

"Got it," Damien yelled from the other side.

I ran around the truck's front. Damien and Alex were standing with the driver's door open.

The man was even bigger than he'd appeared. Damien and I pulled him out of the vehicle and put his arms over our shoulders. We walked him up the causeway. He was a big man, and he wanted to lie down right away.

"Just another few feet. Just a few more," I said.

We got him about twenty feet from the truck and lowered him on the wet grass slope beside the sidewalk, and squatted next to him.

I became aware of approaching sirens.

The front of the truck was now completely on fire. Flames licked the windshield rising higher, and climbed up toward the roof. *It's going to blow*, I thought. *It's really going to blow.*

A fire engine had arrived, the undersides of the tree branches lit by the flashing lights. They shut off the siren, and it was suddenly quiet. Firemen in their baggy coats got out and placed pylons around the truck, and a single fireman extinguished the fire with a hand-held extinguisher.

"He's down here," Alex yelled.

One of them set some type of kit on the sidewalk and crouched down.

"Sir, can you tell us your name?"

"Cook," the man mumbled, barely moving his lips. He mumbled something else, something about mouth and glass.

I glanced again at the truck, the hood now dark and still.

Another fireman covered the man with a blanket and slid off his right shoe and sock. He touched the sole of the foot. "Nod if you can feel that." The man moved his head.

Damien was standing beside me. He leaned over, his hands on his knees, and I noticed a package in his shirt pocket.

"What's this?" I said. I reached in and pulled out a pack of cigarettes.

"Oh... Yeah... Thanks—don't say anything to the others, okay?"

The police were now there and an officer came down and asked who had seen the accident. He was young and had spiked blond hair.

"We were here first," Alex said.

"*Fuck*," Damien said under his breath. "We got to go. Boston Pizza's going to close."

The officer took down our names and our phone numbers and said he had some forms for us to fill out and fax back to him.

"You're not related to Kris Patterson?" he asked as he wrote down my information.

"She's my aunt."

He nodded appreciatively. "She sold us our house."

Not a house; a home.

On the way to Boston Pizza Damien and I made jokes about the accident. Damien said the man's name was Cook, and that's what he would have done if we hadn't saved him. I said that we should have left him and poured barbeque sauce all over the body and watched him cook. The jokes weren't funny, but Damien and I laughed, and Alex, groaning, said that we were *sooo* immature.

Boston Pizza was closed.

We argued about whether to go home or to go somewhere. When we decided on Denny's, Damien complained that he wasn't going to get his beer. He'd saved Cook's life but he wasn't going to get his beer.

Later, when Damien was dead, I would look back on that night as being somehow significant, a night when things almost happened, when our separate lives—Cam's, Damien's, Alex's, and mine—almost converged.

They didn't. But they came close enough that I often imagine what would have happened if they had.

5

Near the end of August Cam began to call again. Usually it would be late at night, and he would sound nervous, and would speak rapidly. The first time this happened I actually thought he was on something.

He said that Damien and I needed to get the band together, we needed to start practicing, we *needed* to record a demo.

He couldn't say how, but soon, "very soon," he was going to meet some *very* important people in *New York,* and he wanted to give them the demo.

And how did I respond?

Lying in bed I'd say, "yeah," or, "sure," not because I believed, or disbelieved what he said. He was my friend, he told me things, I *wanted* to believe him.

"Why didn't you want to come here before?" I asked for the fourth time. For the fourth time, Alex didn't seem to hear my question.

As we walked down the curved cement path to the apartment on Lonsdale, a dropping feeling started in my stomach; I saw the mildew-stained stucco, the broken boards on the railings, the blue flickering light from a television on a third-story apartment ceiling.

An angry male voice came over the intercom. "Yeah, what?"

"It's me," said Alex (her voice higher and cuter than I'd ever heard it.)

The lock buzzed, Alex opened the door, I stepped in behind her.

The bulbs in the lobby light fixtures seemed seventy-five watts too low. There was a brownish stain on the carpet in front of a vinyl sofa. We walked past the elevator and went through a steel door into a hallway. Cigarette burns freckled the green carpets, and a stale smell perfumed the air as if someone had tried to hide bad odors with air freshener. We passed through two more steel doors and down another hall, the muffled sound of heavy metal growing louder as we approached the door of an apartment halfway down it.

Alex knocked. "That was exciting the other night," she said and hummed a verse from Bowie's "Heroes."

She knocked again and looked up at me.

"These are some friends of Leroy's," she said as if in answer to a question that I didn't ask.

She raised her hand to knock again, and the door flew open, the scream of Cannibal Corpse and the smell of marijuana spilling out into the hallway. A girl with dyed-black hair and a scarlet tank top glared at us.

"Yeah?"

"We're Leroy's friends."

"Right," the girl said. She was about the same age as Alex, but her face looked a lot older. Her inverted pentagram necklace glinted in the hall light.

"This is my friend, Trace," Alex said.

"Cool," the girl said.

I nodded, but made sure to keep my hands in my pockets.

She seemed like she wasn't going to move, but then stepped aside.

As we went into the apartment, I started to slip off one of my loafers but noticed that there were no other shoes by the door. I slipped my foot back in.

In front of us was a closed door, and around the corner on the left, the main living room. Directly to my left was a corridor kitchen. Most of the partiers were in the living room, and it didn't take long to notice that they were exclusively twenty-something men and teenage girls.

The kitchen seemed the less crowded of the two rooms, and as Alex went around talking to people I entered the kitchen and stood against the far wall. There was a half-empty bowl of Cheezies on the table and a bottle of Canada Dry ginger ale.

Through the doorway, the left side of the living room was visible. A man in his late twenties lay on the sofa. He was dressed entirely in black and was smoking what appeared to be a cigarette, but had a stoned expression on his face.

Beyond him there were sliding glass doors, and in them my reflection. A dark figure in a skewed square of light.

When I saw Alex again she was standing near the entrance. The man she was talking to wore a wife-beater. He had a goatee that made him look like Pan. A Celtic pattern was tattooed on his bicep. Both his hands were on Alex's bare arms, and Alex was laughing but shaking her head, and he seemed to be trying to convince her to do something.

I was about to approach them when something hit my arm. The man on the sofa through the doorway tried to say something. There was a garbage can beside me. A live cigarette butt lay at my feet. The guy must have been trying to throw it in the garbage. I picked up the butt and put it in the garbage. I imagined it catching fire, the apartment building burning. When I glanced back at the entrance, Alex was gone.

My head was aching. I sat on one of the kitchen chairs and took a couple of deep breaths.

A girl with spiky hair and her left eyebrow pierced came and asked me if I was Redgy. She was quite thin and her midriff was showing, and her belly button was pierced too.

"I don't think so," I said, trying to be witty.

She reached for the bowl of Cheezies in the centre of the table.

"You know someone spat in there," I said.

"I know. That was my friend. So—are you Redgy?"

"No."

The girl tossed the Cheezie into her mouth and folded her arms. "Like, then, who are you?"

It sounded like a simple question, but I couldn't think of the answer. I glanced at the garbage.

"So you're not Redgy?"

"No. I'm not Redgy."

"You have an accent."

I shrugged.

The girl continued to peer at me as she ate the Cheezies.

"Some people think I have an accent," I said.

"What?"

"I said, 'Some people think I have an accent.'"

The girl nodded and tossed another Cheezie in her mouth. With her mouth full, she said, "So where are you from—originally?"

When I said, "Here. North Van," the girl gave me a sarcastic grin. "Seriously, don't bullshit me."

"Nowhere. Here."

She rolled her eyes, and for a moment, was cute.

"Okay, where were you born?"

"Here."

"How about your parents?"

"I don't know. Back east. Somewhere."

"Not England?"

"No."

The girl shook her head. "It's weird. You have like this total British accent."

When I didn't say anything, she said, "You're not bullshitting me?"

I shook my head.

Another girl entered the kitchen. She wore a grey hooded sweat top, with the image of a fish-bone skeleton on the back. She took a Labatt Wildcat from the fridge.

"Here, Kristin, come here," said the girl I'd been talking to. She grabbed the other girl by the sleeve and pulled her over. "Listen to this guy."

The second girl cracked open the can.

"Okay, say something," the first girl said.

"What? What do you want me—"

"Just *anything*. Just say something."

"I don't know. Do you—"

"Make up a story. Tell me why you're here."

"Okay. I. Came with this girl. Alex. And she's this girl I met at the library and—"

"You *see*!" the first girl said to the second girl. "Doesn't he *totally* sound like he has an accent."

"He's faking it," the second girl said. She took a sip of the beer.

"You are faking, aren't you?" said the first one.

I didn't answer. Alex had emerged from the room with the closed door. She was adjusting the strap of her tank top. The man came out, patted her on the shoulder, said something, then went back into the room.

"Alex," I said and waved. Her expression changed.

"Where were you?"

"Nowhere," she said. "Just in there."

"What happened?"

"Nothing."

"What did he do?"

"Nothing. Just some pictures."

"Pictures—"

"Hey, how's it going?" The girl in the fish-bone sweat top hugged Alex, holding the Wildcat off to one side.

When Alex looked back at me, I said, "I think I'm going to go."

"You're not feeling good again?"

"I guess not. I can come and get you later if you want?"

"No. It's okay. I can go too."

Out on the street, I asked Alex again what went on in the bedroom.

"Fuck! Would you give it a rest! *You* wanted to come here."

"I—"

"I'm hungry. I want to go to Burger King."

Neither one of us spoke as we drove there. When we arrived, she was calm again. As I stood in the line-up I found the lit menu board somehow reassuring.

We ordered Whoppers and milkshakes and sat in a booth by the window. It was dark outside and wet.

4:01 A.M.
    "Good evening. You're on Alan Jacobs.
    "I am SO. TIRED. of YOU."

"Okay—"said Alan, unfazed. "Can you be more specific? Is there something in particular that bothers you about my show?"

"YOU are ssPREADING the devil's lies. People are becoming POssessed by listening to your show."

"Well, YOUR'RE listening to my show."

"I'm what?"

"You're listening to my show," Alan continued, deadpan. "Have you become possessed?"

"I need to know the lies that Satan is spreading."

"I find it interesting that you think my show is causing possessions. We rarely talk about religion on this show. In the last month I can think of only ONE show in which Satanism was discussed."

"All of your shows have to do with the Devil and His works. UFOs, aliens, extra-terrestrials—these are all Satan flexing his muscles in the end times."

"So you believe we are in the end times?"

"Yes I do."

"Do you care to put a date on it?"

"The day and the hour are unknown. But the Antichrist has come—"

"Okay, this IS something I want to talk about. This Antichrist, is he around now?"

"He may not be active—but He's here."

"Do you think he's listening to this show?"

"He may very well be."

"Okay—if you're out there, Antichrist, please call in."

My thoughts were racing as I lay in bed that night. I breathed deeply and started to touch myself, tried to focus my thoughts on Alex or Alex's mother or any woman I could think of. But couldn't. I pictured the fat boy at the party astride Luke and the expression on Luke's face as the fat kid drove the tube into his ass. I pictured myself in the room with the closed door. Alex on all fours. The man with the Celtic tattoo telling me what to do.

Just as in the day's of Noah.
Give it time
Just as in the day's of Noah
My little cock can go where big cocks can't
We know who told him to do that
You know, THOSE pesky thoughts

The feeling wasn't going away; the feeling was only intensifying.

I got out of bed. I paced the room. I went down the hall to the kitchen—I wished someone was home, someone to talk to. I thought about calling Kris, but I didn't know where she was, only that she was somewhere in the Okanagan—she'd left no contact information. The air in the kitchen was stupefying. I walked in circles, tried to find a cold patch of tile to stand on, then went outside by the pool. The air was cooler there. It was quiet too. I looked up at the black shape of the mountain under the blue sky, the dim glimmer of the Skyride going down its face, the lights of the chalet at the top illuminating the low-flying clouds like the glow from the mouth of a volcano to which people were sacrificed; then out over the treetops at the shimmer of the city and the harbour. There was a breeze. For a moment I thought I was going to be okay. But the feeling returned. It wasn't as strong as before though, and I went back inside, leaving the door ajar, and turned on the TV. It was tuned to MuchMusic, a Rusty video playing. The remote sat on the coffee table and I reached to switch the channel, but the song came to the chorus. Unlike the verse, the chorus was poppy and catchy, and as I continued to watch, the feeling gradually subsided.

The video was a parody of *The Midnight Cowboy*, and I thought of Joe Buck.

When the video ended, I realized that it was going to be okay, that I was going to be okay.

Damien was at the pool table in the centre of the room when I stepped out of the elevator. He was leaning across the table, throwing the one ball against the bumper and catching it when it bounced back. The room had a high ceiling and there was a skylight: there were bars on the skylight. This—Damien had once told me—was the ward reserved for the seriously disturbed.

When he'd called the previous night, I knew something was really wrong because he'd done something that he had never done before: he *didn't* make me guess where he was—he just told me.

There were problems with his medication, and they were going to try something different. But what most worried him was another patient. The patient, an older woman with a "Woodstock Forever" T-shirt, had threatened to cut his head off.

"Hey," he said, noticing me. He dropped the ball in a pocket.

"Do you want to play?"

He shook his head and stepped back from the table.

"I brought you something—" I'd thought he'd catch on right away.

He looked puzzled.

"A *gift*."

Still a blank expression. But then he smiled wanly. "Oh yeah. Yeah, thanks. But I can't do that. They think that's what might be interfering with my medication. Sorry."

"No problem," I said, shrugging.

In the room to the right of us, there was a woman in an easy chair watching television. She had her back to us, and she seemed to be tearing something in her hands.

"So is that her?" I said, not actually thinking that it was the woman he'd told me about.

"Shhhh," Damien said, suddenly very nervous. "Keep your voice down."

The woman looked to be in her late forties. She wore a green terry-towel housecoat, and had very short hair that appeared to have been dyed orange.

I couldn't see from where I was standing whether she was wearing her "Woodstock Forever" T-shirt.

"Come in here," he said. He led me into the kitchen area. From the fridge he took out a small cup of Dairyland raspberry cocktail.

"You want one?"

Ignoring the sign that said that drinks were for patients only, I nodded.

"I haven't seen these in years," I said, peeling off the foil cover. "This girl I used to play with, her mother would always—"

"I'm *not* joking," said Damien. "I'm really scared of that woman."

"The woman in there?"

He nodded and told me that that morning she'd been standing over his bed with a pair of scissors.

I laughed.

"Fuck—I'm serious!" he said. "She said all this crazy shit. Like she knew I was a dirty pervert. That I was masturbating about her and she—she was going to fucking cut *it* off."

It was difficult not to laugh again. "Then why don't you just tell the nurse?" I said.

"They don't do fucking anything," he said desperately. "They'll just talk about adjusting my medication."

We were still talking about the woman when a male nurse approached us. He was pushing a cart with paper cups on top.

He checked a list on a clipboard, then said in a saccharine tone. "Okay, Daniel. Time for the ol' *medication*."

Damien took the paper cup from the nurse and shook it. He turned it on its side and shook it again. The nurse just stood there, watching.

"What's this?" Damien said, pointing to a large blue pill.

"Daniel, that's *your* medication."

"This is Androcur. I'm not supposed to be on it. They changed my medication."

"You just take them and I'll ask Doctor Bennett."

There was a garbage can beside us. Damien dropped the cup in it.

"Oookay Danny." The nurse wrote something on his clipboard. "Have a nice day."

"That's what I fucking hate about this place," Damien whispered when the man was gone. "Now I'm going to be in all this shit. Fuck!"

After that, he wanted me to leave. I said that I could stay and help him talk to the doctor. But he said it was better if I wasn't there.

I tried to figure out what I should do. It was hard to know how seriously to take what Damien had said about the other patient. He had a habit of exaggerating things, and I didn't even know if he really believed what he said, or just wanted to shock me.

The last thing that I remember was his feet. I was staring down as he told me about how the nurse was a "fag" and probably wanted him to get killed anyway: his feet, in the paper hospital slippers, lined up perfectly with a seam in the linoleum floor.

At the end of that week I received a very strange phone call from Cam. Unlike the other calls, which came late at night, this one came in the afternoon. For most of it he just whimpered on the other end of the line, saying that a fortune cookie had said that it was going to happen. The question of what was never answered. The only response I got to any question was that he was tired of being so insecure.

After about five minutes of this, the line went dead.

"Are you there? Are you there?" I heard the click that really meant the line was dead.

I was on the portable phone and I went back to my bedroom and hung up. For a few minutes I just stood there, listening to the muted sound of the rain on the shed's roof—the hollow smacking sound each drop made as it hit the plastic cover—then walked back down the hall and into the living room. It had become dark while I'd been talking on the phone. The streetlight outside was now on, and coming to the window, I noticed that the light made the wet black surface of the driveway shine.

What was I supposed to do?

My hands felt shaky as I flipped through the stations. The rain had let up outside. I turned my wipers off and slowed for the intersection, images of a pedestrian's yellow coat and a red stop sign floating on the wet pavement. Kitchener was the next street. I turned right. There was no parking in front of Maria's house, and I cruised down one street and over another, and finding a spot, pulled into it.

As I walked back, I kept telling myself to be calm, I didn't know for sure that it had been Maria.

The week before I'd gone to The Railway to see a band play and was certain that I'd seen Maria in a booth with Sadie's friend Hugh, at least I thought I had. It was hard to tell because she'd had her face turned to him. But he had *that* sport coat over her lap, and *that* hand doing something under it. I'd been afraid she'd see me, and had gone to the washroom before I could make sure. When I'd come out, they were no longer there, but I couldn't find any couple in the club that looked like the couple I'd seen.

At the gate in front of the house, I hesitated. I remembered the evening that I first unlatched it. The pink twilight. The warmth of the air. The cat weaving between our legs.

The front room was dark. I tried to see if anyone was in there, then opened the gate and climbed to the porch and knocked. Cuban music came faintly from the other side of the door. I stood on my tiptoes. Down the hall light shone from the kitchen. I knocked again. A dark figure appeared in the lit doorway. I thought it was Fernando, then that it wasn't, then saw that it was. He'd grown a beard.

The music became louder as the door opened.

"Sorry—"

He shook his head.

"Is Maria in?"

"She. She gone."

"When is she going to be home?"

"She. She moved."

"Where?"

He shook his head.

I remained standing there, so finally he said, "Wait." He gestured with his hand for me to stay outside. He closed the door and disappeared through the lit doorway down the hall.

When he didn't come back right away, I wondered if he was going to return. The kitchen doorway darkened with shadow, and he appeared and walked toward the door and opened it.

He handed me a slip of paper. "This. Her address."

"Thank you," I said. He'd scratched the address out faintly in pencil.

I walked in the direction he'd pointed. I didn't know the area, but I hoped that unlike the streets in North Van, these streets connected.

Light spilled out of the pizzeria at the corner of Commercial and Kitchener. In the steamed window a couple my age was holding hands.

The next street was the street written on the piece of paper. I turned right and began to check the house numbers. The house whose number matched the number on the paper was almost identical to the house I'd just left: three stories high, a porch in front, a garden fenced with wrought iron.

I opened the gate (also identical) and walked through the garden. The trees were still dripping from the rain earlier. Soon it would be fall and they would be losing their leaves. I climbed to the porch and knocked. A joke Maria had told me came back to me: *Kill me, just don't leave me.*

With the ringing of a bell and squeaking, the door swung back.

A woman in her early thirties peered out.

"Sorry. Someone said a Maria, a Mexican girl, lived here."

The woman turned and shouted into the house. "Maria, someone's here to see you." She did this so casually

I wondered if other men had come to the door asking for Maria.

When she turned back, her bangs fell in her eyes. She used her little finger and cleared them out of the way. The other hand was still holding the door. Her bare legs and the oversized UBC sweat top made her look young, but there were lines around her eyes.

"You a friend of Maria's?"

I said that I was.

A vehicle splashed by slowly on the street behind me. Someone inside the house was playing U2's "One." The woman leaned out the door and stared at the dark sky.

"Has it stopped raining?"

"Yes."

"Almost feels like fall."

"Yeah."

She hollered inside again, "Maria."

"Hey, where are you going?" she said. "She's coming."

But my right foot was already on the edge of the top step. "I forgot something. My car, it's parked in front of a fire hydrant. I'll be back in a sec."

3:43 A.M.

"These possessions... how do they occur?"

"They can occur in a whole number of ways. They—"

"Can... Sorry. Go on."

"They can occur in a whole number of ways," said the guest. *He was soft spoken, with a light, Irish accent. "But one precondition in about ninety percent of the exorcisms I've been involved in is loneliness. The demon approaches the person when they are alone and cut off from people. And then once the person is possessed the demon, or demons—quite often there is more than one—they will keep that person alone."*

"So they get you alone, and they keep you alone."

"Exactly."

"For those of you who have just tuned in, I am speaking to Caleb Collins, a retired priest and exorcist, and we're talking about demon possession in general, and in particular, the case of Mitchell Schrader, the elderly man whose decapitated body was found in his scooter in a field in Wisconsin. So, Father, you were saying earlier that you think whoever did this to Mitchell Schrader was demon possessed."

"It's very likely…"

I lowered the volume and turned on my back. I had closed the drapes because outside was a full moon. Above me the ceiling's exposed wood beams looked shadowy in the green light of the stereo's dial, and I imagined what it would be like if they came down on me.

I was in my room packing, getting ready for the trip to Harrison when the doorbell rang.

"Who is it?" I asked.

"Me—Cam."

I was a bit surprised when I opened the door. Cam stepped in. He looked somehow bigger than the last time I'd seen him. His hair and leather jacket were wet.

"Sorry I didn't call first. I was afraid they were listening."

"Who?"

He panted. "I'll tell you in a sec. Do you have a towel?"

When I returned with the towel, Cam had taken off his Adidas runners and was coming toward me.

He snatched the towel and wiped his head. In my room I sat at the desk. He got up on the bed opposite and leaned against the wall.

The desk light was on. His face, I remember, looked tired and haggard in the light.

"Put some music on."

"What do you want?"

"I don't care. Just put something on."

That week I'd been getting ready for my move back to UBC, but my old stereo was still hooked up. I dug through the CDs strewn on the floor. I intended to play *Zeppelin I* or Aerosmith's *Pump,* but found *Appetite for Destruction*, and put it on.

Seconds of silence. Slash's delayed riff.

Cam grinned as the drums and bass guitar entered.

As Axl Rose muttered something about God, I'm sure Cam and I were thinking of the same memory: the bus ride to outdoor school in Grade 11 when Cam first heard the album on Damien's Walkman.

"Do you want something to drink?" I said.

"What do you have?"

"Beer?"

"Yeah."

I got two large bottles of Becks—the 710ml ones—and as we sat in my room drinking them, Cam told me what he came here to tell me. None of it surprised me.

Two weeks before he'd had an altercation with the homestay parents of the Brazilian girl. When he went to visit her, the homestay parents wouldn't let him see her. They accused him of calling the house ten or twelve times a day, and at two and three in the morning.

"That wasn't me," Cam told me, "that was that fucker in Brazil, her old boyfriend."

They'd told him that the girl was scared of him. When Cam tried to enter the house, the homestay father stopped him and the police were called. But Cam wouldn't leave, and they took him down to the station, and now he had some sort of restraining order.

139

"That's how you're going to help me," Cam said, his tone already suggesting it was something that I wouldn't be agreeable to.

"The police think the girl went back to Brazil. But she didn't. She's still in Vancouver."

"How do you know?"

"Because *we* tricked them. I knew that they wouldn't let me out when she was still here. So I told her to pretend to go home."

"When did you tell her that?"

"When I was in the jail. I wrote her a letter telling her to tell them that she was going home and then wait for me to contact her."

"Did she write back?"

"I told her not to. It was too dangerous. I told her to wait for me to contact her."

"How do you know she got the letter?"

"I know."

"How?"

"I wrote two letters. The first one was in English and I gave it to this 'counsellor' to give to her. But the counsellor opened it and refused to give it to her. So the second one I wrote completely in Portuguese and gave it to my sister to give her friend. I'm sure that that one got through because no one ever mentioned it and the police believed me when I said that I hadn't tried to contact her anymore."

"So what do you want me to do?"

"First I want you to go to her friend's homestay house and give her friend a letter I have. Then I want you to go to the Cambie next Friday and give the girl a letter."

"How do you know she's going to be there?"

"The letter you're going to give the friend is going to tell her to be there."

"Why do *I* have to give it to her? Can't you do it?"

He let out an exasperated sigh. "I told you—the restraining order. I *cannot* contact the girl."

"Even the friend?"

"Even the friend."

I asked him if this was a good idea.

"Why? Why isn't it a good idea?"

I didn't say anything.

"They're not going to catch me. Trust me. The girl and I have a *special* bond."

I remained silent.

"No one's going to catch me."

When I still didn't answer, he said, "No one can stop me."

When Cam and I got outside it was night. The rain had stopped. The night air was cold. A long white gleam stretched down the road from the light at the end of the cul-de-sac. The faint roar of water going over the dam half a mile up the canyon came from the distance.

My canvas shoes were soaking by the time I got to the car. Cam started the engine and the wipers cleared the beads of water from the windshield. Condensation rushed across the glass, then slowly receded.

I thought about why I was doing this.

Nothing he had said could possibly be true—Cam could not write Portuguese, his sister had not given the letter to the girl, the girl was not still in Vancouver, the government was not looking for him.

But he was alone with these thoughts, and I knew what it was like to be alone with one's thoughts.

"Have you talked to Damien?"

"Yeah, last week."

"He's not doing well?"

I laughed. "He thinks someone's trying to kill him at the hospital."

"Tell him next time you talk to him that I *like* him. That I don't hold anything against him."

"Sure." I said.

As he said these things the Beemer careened around one blind corner after another, heading toward the turn off to Edgemont. The road ran along the eastern edge of the canyon, and across it the lights of West Van houses hung in the drenched darkness.

Cam turned on the stereo and Rage Against The Machine's "Killing in the Name" throbbed from the back speakers. When we got to Edgemont Village the streets were deserted, the street lights shone eerily and a neon sign saying "Drugs" glowed on the Pharmasave's roof.

"You know what my sister said to me tonight?" Cam said, turning down the stereo's volume.

My eyes were fixed to the sign. "What?"

"She asked if I was taking my medication."

"Yeah?"

"My *baby sister*!"

I waited for him to say more, to elaborate. But again, except for the clacking of the dry wipers, the car was silent.

When we reached Grand Boulevard, my nerves were bad. I tried to swallow, I tried to take only large breaths.

Cam turned down a side street and coasted past a one-storey stucco bungalow where the front light was on. "That's the house," he said, pointing.

Two more houses down he pulled to the curb. Leaning across me he took a sealed white envelope from the glove compartment.

"What if she's not there?"

He bit his bottom lip, hard.

"You don't want me to give it to them, the homestay parents?"

"No," he said.

My wet shoes squished on the wet pavement as I walked back to the girl's house. Waiting for someone to come to the door, I noticed I'd squeezed the envelope too tightly. I tried to straighten it. There was still no response after a minute and I peered through the panel of frosted glass to the side of the door and saw in the distance a diffused patch of light. A blurred shadow moved across it. Footsteps came. The glass grew dark. The lock clicked, the door squeaked on its hinges.

The woman looking at me was squat and shapeless.

"Is Adriana home?"

She continued studying me. There were prints of windmills on the dress, and her face had been scarred by acne. "Who may I say is calling?"

"Um, Richard," I said. It was the first name that came to mind, and I remember that it almost made me laugh.

"I'm afraid she's out at the moment."

I asked if she knew when Adriana might return.

"It should be soon. Is there something I can give her?"

"Uh—"

"Or maybe you can come back later?"

"Yeah. Maybe that's better."

I was at least at the end of the driveway before I heard the door close.

"Well—what happened?" Cam asked when I got in the car.

"She wasn't home."

"Did you leave the letter?"

"Did you want me to?"

He looked at his watch. "Who was there?"

"The homestay mother, I guess... I told her my name was 'Richard.'"

"*Richard.*" Cam laughed, and I laughed. I guess he and I both found the name funny. "How did she act?"

"I think she was suspicious. Do you want to wait?"

"We can catch her even before she gets to the house."

"Sure," I said.

The rain began again, drop by drop stippling the windshield. The drops ran together. Through the streaked glass, the road distorted and blurred. At one point Cam turned the wipers on, the radio blasting out the middle of "Semi-Charmed Life."

He turned off the motor and it was again silent, except for the steadily loudening sound of the rain on the vinyl roof.

"What if she called the cops?" I finally said.

"Do you think she did?"

"She was suspicious."

The sound of the rain grew louder, almost sizzling.

"Fuck!"

We both laughed. I guess he and I were thinking the same thing—how it'd appear to the police if they found two men sitting outside a female student's homestay house at ten o'clock at night in a dark car.

"We're fucked up."

"Yeah—we're fucked," I said. We laughed again.

"All I want to do is talk to her."

But to pay just to talk to someone...

"It looks bad," I said.

Cam now really began to laugh.

"I think we'd better go," he said.

"Otherside" blared on as the motor turned over. Cam shifted into first and pulled away from the curb.

As he drove me back up Grand Boulevard toward the entrance to the freeway, I thought that I should feel better, that I should feel relieved that nothing had happened.

The street lights glided by overhead, one after another, lurid and faint. When we reached the on-ramp to the highway, I heard myself say, "Go back."

Cam turned, he kept turning, he did a U-turn and started to drive back down Grand Boulevard.

"Are we going back?" I asked him.

"We've got to, *right?*"

I tried to speak.

"Right?" he shouted.

I grasped the door handle and pushed myself back in the seat. "Yeah."

Three minutes later I was in front of the house again. Cam had parked beside a tall, dark hedge a block away. Giving me the letter, he'd said, "Tell her not to open it. It's private."

"Sure," I'd said, knowing that I wasn't going to say anything so suspicious.

The house looked warm and dry. To anyone seeing me standing there—a soaking wet man in the middle of the road at night—I must have looked insane, like one of those maniacs in the slasher films waiting outside the teenage girl's house.

The letter tucked under my arm, I again walked up the driveway and climbed the chipped cement steps and rang the doorbell. I wiped the dripping bangs from my eyes. There was a siren far off and I thought the woman might have called the police. I got ready to run. The siren grew louder, then faded into the sound of the downpour.

Blurred shadows were moving behind the frosted glass. They became larger, and more focused.

I tried to make my hair neat, I tried to look friendly.

The lock clicked. The door was pulled back.

The same woman.

"I'm sorry to bother you again," I began.

This time she was more nervous. "That's—okay," she said.

"Is Adriana now home?"

"No, she isn't. But I'm sure she'll be here any moment. You're wet. Do you want to come in and wait?" Down the hall behind her, a man sat at the table in the kitchen watching.

"Um. No. I better go. But can I leave this for her?"

The woman took the crumpled letter.

"Thank you," I said. "Tell her I'll call her tomorrow."

"Okay," the woman said.

Trying not to rush but rushing, I stepped down the cement stairs and walked up the driveway, then down the dark street toward the car.

When I was sure I was out of the view of the house, I ran.

6

Kris came out of the washroom, her hair wrapped in a bath towel. "Don't just stand there. Be useful."

"What do you want me to do?"

She glared at me. "Do I have to tell you? There's luggage to be loaded."

"Is it ready?" I asked.

Kris only looked at me and shook her head. She turned and went back into the washroom.

A travel bag and a suitcase stood by the door in the front hall. I tried to pick up both. The suitcase was too heavy so I took the bag out first.

The clear weather that morning made me feel better. The previous night I hadn't really slept. I would wake up every hour or so with a shaking feeling deep inside. At one point I turned on the light and looked at my hands, hoping to see physical proof that something was wrong with me.

There was an autumn coldness in the morning air, and as I walked back to the house, I realized that I was looking forward to my return to UBC in a week's time—the crisp mornings with steam rising off the pool at the Aquatic

Centre, the men in Plant Operation uniforms clearing the lawns with their leaf blowers, the fresh girls in their tank tops and shorts.

When I stepped inside the house, Kris was waiting. "You didn't see my travel bag, the one with the fish logo on it?"

"I—" I looked outside.

"Go get it! I need it!" she shouted.

"You said—"

"I said 'suitcases.' Not 'bag.' And take this one when you go. I suppose I have to tell you that."

Kris remained silent for the first forty minutes of the drive. I slouched back in the passenger seat with my knees pressed against the dashboard. I tried to avoid any thoughts of the "vacation." This yearly family reunion at Harrison had been fun during the time when my grandparents had gone. But since they stopped going, and it was only Becky and Kris, it had become tension-filled, a sort of morbid reenactment of the previous years' situations and conflicts. The only thing I was looking forward to was seeing my cousin Emily. The previous summer was the first time that she'd been old enough to hang out with, and we had played pinball in the games room, working together by telling each other which target to shoot for, and had ended up getting the highest score.

I was still thinking about this when Kris said, "Did you happen to see the weather forecast?"

"No."

"I thought they said we were going to have sun."

"I don't know."

"It doesn't look good."

Far ahead in the blue distance, rising above the silvery grey cloud, was the dome of Mount Baker.

Four more miles passed in silence. Then Kris said, "How's your friend doing?"

"Which one?" I asked, but already suspecting which one she was interested in.

"The one I met earlier this summer."

"Damien?"

"Not *him*," she said grimacing. "Good-looking, tall."

"Cam?"

"Was that his name?"

When I said "Yes," she nodded, as if in agreement with her own thoughts.

I switched on the radio and tuned through the stations until I found one playing Blind Melon's "Galaxie." The station had static, and I got it as clear as possible before settling back in the seat.

"Do we need that on?" Kris said after about a minute.

I waited until the end of the chorus, then turned it off. I took my knapsack from the backseat and dug out my Discman. As I was putting the headphones on, I heard Kris say something about me having a lot of repressed anger that I needed to deal with. Spacehog's first album was in the Discman and I turned the volume up loud and tried to focus on the chiming sound of the guitars, then the bass line.

As had happened in previous years, Kris's war with the hotel began almost as soon as we arrived. It was lunch time and the desk clerk informed Kris that our rooms would not be ready until four.

"Four! What type of hotel has a four o'clock check in time?"

The clerk, a short young woman with her hair tied tight in a bun and a hawk-like nose, responded by aggressively typing something on her computer. "Let me. Check one thing."

"I *knew* that couldn't be right," Kris said in a softened tone.

"I'm sorry. We are busy this weekend and the room won't be ready for at least another hour. But the concierge can store your luggage for you. And you are welcome to use any of our facilities."

"How can I use your facilities," Kris said, "when I can't even change into my bathing suit?"

"There are change rooms at the pool."

"Great! I pay three hundred dollars, and then have to use public washrooms to change!" She turned to me. "I can see this is the last year *we'll* be coming *here*," she hissed loud enough for the desk clerk to hear. She turned back to the clerk and said, "I think I'm going to need to speak to the manager."

Twenty minutes later Kris and I followed a bellhop to rooms on the fifth floor of the West Tower, Kris again in a good mood.

"These hotels," Kris joked, "the stress they put you through just to check into your room, you need a vacation afterwards."

The bellhop let out a nervous laugh.

Our rooms were next to each other on the poolside of the tower. I carried my knapsack into my room, and Kris disappeared into her room with the bellhop and her luggage. When the door swung shut, I was startled by the silence. I pulled open the drapes and the sliding door, and stepped out on the balcony. Down below, middle-aged bathers were already filling the adult hot pool. On the other side of the footbridge, children were frolicking in the Family Pool. Emily didn't appear to be anywhere.

When Kris knocked on the door I was lying on the bed. I blinked a couple of times and sat up.

"Are you in there?" I heard her shout.

I walked over to the door. "Coming," I shouted.

Kris had already changed from the slacks. She wore a purple long dress with black geometric patterns on it.

"That was a nice bellhop," she said.

"Really?"

"He's going to UBC too." She stared past me into the room. "Can I come in?"

I stepped aside. She went into the washroom, flipped on the lights, studied the room, then flipped off the lights and went out into the main room.

"Isn't it the same as yours?"

"Roughly," she said still looking around.

I waited for her to suggest that we switch rooms.

"I guess it's the same." She looked back at me, then away. "Um," she said as if trying to remember what she wanted to say. "Are you coming down to the lobby?"

"Is Aunt Rebecca and Emily here yet?"

"I don't know. I expect they'll wait for us in the lobby when they come. Are you coming down?"

"In a bit. I just want to have a rest now."

I lay down on the bed again and thought about what I wanted to do. After fifteen minutes I couldn't think of anything.

Kris was sitting in the armchair beside the large flagstone fireplace, with Aunt Becky on the adjacent sofa. They leaned over the end table, talking. I sat on the hearth in front of them but neither one noticed me. An elderly woman was doing a crossword at the other end of the sofa, and next to her a girl in her early teens dressed like a Goth stared glumly at the carpet. Far down the lobby, a couple in bathrobes stopped to read something on the wall and the woman slid her hand into his back pocket.

"Trace," Aunt Becky said. "There you are!"

"He *has* changed," she said to Kris as she stood up to hug me. "How's my nephew?"

"Fine," I said, feeling her small breasts push into me.

"Jack would be proud," she said and stepped back to look me over. "Em, aren't you going to say hello to your cousin?"

I glanced around. Becky was glaring at the girl in Goth wear. "You'll have to excuse her, Trace. She's in the *too-cool-for-school* phase."

The girl's expression soured.

"Come on. Get up. Give your cousin a hug."

The girl, after another second of resistance, threw herself to her feet, almost violently, and staggered forward. She reached with her right hand, her arms still pressed to her sides, her fingers limp. The hand in my hand felt like a dead person's.

The gray light over the top of the curtains made spike-shapes on the ceiling. I got up and went out on the balcony. The air out there was cold. Over the hill the sky was a pale blue and three bathers were out down below.

Though I wanted to go straight into the hot water, I made myself swim first. A white towel was spread out on one of the lounge chairs, but no one was around. The water wasn't as cold as I expected, and by the time I reached the shallow end only my face felt chilled. I pushed off the wall and did a crawl back toward the deep end, halfway down flipping on my back and gazing up at the morning sky, listening to the eerie muffled sound my kicks made, and when I stopped, what sounded like bubbles rising. The image of Paul Ramsey's bloated corpse floating came into my head. I pushed it out with Jason Voorhees'. *Kill her, Mommy! Kill her. Don't let her get away.* And laughed. I neared the wall and stuck out my hand and grabbed the edge. Beyond the fence a steep slope rose, covered in trees. The leaves had already begun to change. Fleetingly, the feeling of being here as a child returned—the enjoyable feeling of being frightened by the thought that the Sasquatch could come out of those trees in the night, come lurching across the lawn to the ground floor room my parents always had.

I lingered on the edge long enough to catch my breath, then did a front crawl to the shallow end.

It wasn't until I had got out and was relaxing in the hot pool, my head rested on the stones as my legs floated on the surface, watching the swaths of steam rise and disappear in the morning air, that I realized I was actually enjoying the vacation. I hadn't wanted to come here this year. But the change of scenes had been good. The trip with Cam in the car was a long ways away.

I was still sitting there when I heard the approaching sound of female voices.

"O*kay*—Emily, but what do you want me to do about it?"

She and Aunt Becky appeared on the foot bridge.

"Put the towel over there," Becky said. She was wearing a yellow one piece, and I thought about the sensation of her breasts pressing against me.

Emily tiptoed to a large rock by the edge of the pool. She set the towel down on it, and undid the belt of her bathrobe.

"Aww," Aunt Becky gasped, stretching and stepping down the stairs into the hot pool.

"Good morning. You're up bright and early."

I nodded.

"I guess Kris isn't up yet?"

"No."

"Em, Trace is here."

Emily had gotten into the pool behind Becky. She was crouching low in the water.

"You disappeared early last night," Becky said to me.

"I was tired from the drive."

"You're lucky you didn't have Em here for a bed partner. She was up till one watching—What was that movie called?"

Emily said something. She was standing behind Becky.

"What was it—for heaven sakes, stop mumbling."

"Anyway," Becky said turning back to me. "This movie was *weird*."

I nodded, trying not to look like I agreed or disagreed.

Becky glided over to the far side of the pool and lay back in the water.

Emily crouched in the middle of the pool, holding her arms tightly in front of her. She looked more normal than when I'd seen her the previous night. She didn't have any make-up on, and she wore a navy two-piece bathing suit.

"So was the movie good?" I said.

She didn't seem to hear me, and I said a bit louder, "Was the movie good?"

Not looking at me, she frowned. "Not really," she said. She went to the side and sat on the ledge. She kept both her arms crossed in front of her.

"Just something to do?"

She reached with her right hand and pulled up the cup of her bathing top and re-crossed her arms. She shrugged. "I guess."

At lunch Emily had put make-up on again, but it wasn't as severe as it had been the day before; she looked less like Marilyn Manson and more like the Emily I remembered. For most of the meal Kris told Becky that the food prices were ridiculous. After we finished, I asked Emily if she wanted to see if they still had the pinball machine.

I wasn't sure if the shrug she gave me was a "yes" or a "no." I stood up and put my napkin on the table. But as I pushed out my chair, Emily rose too.

We remained silent as we went downstairs. I had to stop at the front desk to change a five dollar bill into quarters. As we waited for the concierge, Emily stared at the floor and stepped on the lace of her right shoe with her left shoe, and tried to pull it loose.

Nothing had changed in the games room—the same ping-pong table in the middle of the room; the same shuffleboard markings on the floor by the far wall; even the fluorescent lighting tubes seemed burned out in the same places.

The pinball machine was still to the right of the door, and I could tell immediately by the checker marking that it was still Williams' "Diner."

My right pocket was lumpy with quarters, and I took one out.

"Do you want to go first?"

Emily looked glumly at the machine. "You go. I'll just watch."

I dropped in a quarter and the machine came to life, the streamlined American-style diner illuminated on the back box, "Credit 1" flashing in digital writing near the bottom. I poked the button on the front and a steel ball popped into the ball lane.

I rested my hands on the side of the machine and fluttered my fingers. "Sure you don't want to go first?"

She shook her head.

I pulled back the plunger and let go. The ball shot up the lane and disappeared under some ramps at the top of the field, then reappeared, and rolled through a gate and hit the top bumper.

"Order up!"

"Do you remember how to play this?"

The ball ricocheted between the three top bumpers, rolled out and sped down the field.

"Could you please give to me a Hot Dog and a Root Beer."

"Don't you remember anything?"

She only shrugged.

One of the five customers pictured in the centre of the playing field lit up: a man, wearing a turban, called Haji.

I let the flipper down, then fired. The ball hit the drop targets for both the chilli and the hamburger.

"I think I'm supposed to knock all these down."

"What's the point?" she asked, as I dropped the target for the hot dog.

"Of this game?"

"Anything—what's the point?"

I tried for the iced tea, but missed.

I lost that game. I played another. I played two more without either one of us speaking.

"I know whatever I tell you, you're going to tell her."

"Who?" The ball rolled between my flippers.

No response.

"Your mother?"

A nod.

The ball shot into a ball lane.

"I barely know her," I said. I slapped the plunger. As the ball bounced back and forth at the top of the field I remembered that I was supposed to light all three entrance gates. The ball settled in the left one and I used the flipper buttons to take the light off that gate.

"*Okay*," she said, making it sound like a threat.

The ball rolled into the first bumper.

"Then don't tell her what my friend and I are planning to do."

"What—what's that?" I tried to sound calm.

She laughed.

The ball hit the flipper and rolled down it, half up the inner lane. I had the flipper raised and the ball came back down and went over to the left side.

"I'll have the Texas Chilli and Fries!"

My finger crushed the button, holding the ball still.

"Do you mean like—" Her manner was freaking me out. It reminded me of Cam's at the beach.

"Hurry up, partner!"

"Nevermind."

"Have you, have you talked to someone?"

"You sound like *her!*"

"What? What do you mean?"

Order up!

I'd like an Iced Tea and a Frankfurter.

"Like some *pervert* sucking on me is going to help me?!"

My finger slipped. The ball dropped off the flipper and disappeared into the dead ball slot.

Andale! Andale!

Emily had turned and walked out.

I stood standing at the machine. "Game Over," flashed on the back box.

I walked into the hallway. I looked back and forth. It was silent except for the churning of the ice maker.

Only the top of the hill now had sunlight, the rest of it in shade. High voices of children and the murmur of people came up from below. I picked up the hotel glass at the side of the chair and finished the watery dregs of a gin and tonic. The 375ml of Gordon's, which I'd bought after finishing pinball, was now almost empty.

Give it time.

Someone knocked. I hesitated, not knowing if it was someone else's door or my own. Kris shouted.

"Coming," I shouted back.

Standing, suddenly realizing how wasted I was, I giggled.

"Ba, ba, ba, Can't You Hear Me Knocking…" I staggered inside and through the room. At the door I turned the handle and pulled—the chain was on. "Wait a second." I reclosed the door and slid the chain off, amused that I couldn't remember putting it in place.

Kris came in the room. "They're gone."

"What?"

"They're *gone*." She started to pace.

I closed the door and locked it.

"Where?"

"Home. I don't know. Back to Kelowna."

The room wobbled. I lowered myself into the chair at the desk and slid down in it. Any good feeling had now gone.

"Did Emily… Did something happen?"

Kris threw up her hands.

"They just said they were going home?"

"They didn't say anything."

"How do you know?"

"I just talked to the front desk. They checked out—have you been drinking?"

"Uh…" I tried to remember where I put the Gordon's bottle.

"I guess we had some kind of fight." Kris said still walking from one side of the room to the other.

"Becky and you?"

"She told me she'd found Emily taking some of her pills out of her cabinet. I said the girl looks a bit messed up—not exactly like that. I said something like… like she looks troubled. That's the word I used, 'troubled.'"

"And?"

"Aaand—then she suddenly started going on about all this stuff from our childhood. How I thought I was better than other people. How Janet and I thought we were so special. How our parents favoured us. How she never got anything. How Janet and I wrecked everything. How *she* never had three divorces—"

Kris continued to speak. I was glad that I wasn't sober.

When she finally stopped, she laughed and said, "Also—they think you're gay."

I pretended to laugh.

"Anyway," she said standing, wiping her eyes. She let out a loud sigh.

"Did she go to a psychiatrist?"

Aunt Kris stared at me. "What?"

"Did she go to a doctor?"

"She told you, huh?" Kris said. "I guess the guy did something… inappropriate. They're going somewhere else now."

"Anyway, nothing to do now I guess but enjoy *our* vacation," she said. She smiled as if trying to keep tears out of her eyes. "I made reservations at The Copper Room for seven.

"Okay," I said.

She blew her nose in the washroom and left.

The next day I slept as long as possible. When I woke it was late morning. I put on my trunks and went to the pools. There weren't many people in the large one. But it wasn't the same as the previous morning. I didn't have the clean empty feeling after I swam. After two laps, bumping into someone on one of the laps, I stayed in the deep end and watched the other guests.

The sun was bright and the glare from the water made me squint. A boy of about nine or ten chased an older girl with a Super Soaker water pistol on the pool deck. She was eleven or twelve, and taller than the boy, and something about how she ran screaming reminded me of how Emily had been two years before.

As more people arrived the pool became too crowded for me to swim, and I got out and went to the hot pool. It too was crowded. It was hard to find a place to sit and I crouched in the middle. The leaves on the white-barked tree beside the pool were already about to turn yellow. A few dead leaves drifted on the surface of the pool. I thought of the time I'd come up here two years ago, the summer my grandfather died, the Labor Day Weekend before my Grade-11 year. The night I returned to Vancouver my house had been egged by Patrick Ian and his friends. Cam had told him that I'd said he and the head of the basketball team were bum buddies, and egging my house was his revenge. Even though I didn't like it at the time, it was now a good memory.

When I thought that I was hot enough that the walk through the cold air wouldn't bother me, I went to the change room, showered, and dried off in the sauna. I was lying in there when I became aroused by the idea of me and someone being alone in there and what we could do, and I went back to the room. But when I got up there, another scenario entered my head.

Afterwards, expecting that Kris was already up and was looking for me, I searched the lounge and The Lakeview Terrace. When I didn't find her in either place, I had the crazy thought that she might have left without me. I checked that the car was still in the parking lot. The air was crisp outside; the sky was clear. I decided to take a walk after breakfast, so I went back to my room for my UBC sweat top. On the way back to the Lakeside Terrace, I paused by Kris's room and put my ear to the door. A hum of a blow dryer came from inside, and I heard her cough. She would probably go to the Lakeside Terrace for brunch; and without knocking on the door I went down to the restaurant and got a table for two. It was by the window. The maples across the road were swaying in the wind, the leaves flying off them. I adjusted the cutlery and waited for Kris.

When the waiter returned, he asked if I was going to have the buffet—he was a stout man with strawberry-blond hair and a walrus mustache, and I recognized him from previous visits.

"No. Can I just have a side of bacon and side of hash browns and a glass of orange juice?"

"As you wish."

The lake, which was large and surrounded by mountains, was very dark and blue—it looked cold. A local person had told us that it was colder than one expected and that people often drowned in it. A large island sat three miles out, and I wondered if you could swim to it. On the shore, a woman in cotton jersey and jeans was walking a small dog. Something about her style reminded me of photographs I'd seen of my parents.

The waiter soon returned with my bacon and hash browns.

"Are you alone?" he asked as he set the plate on the table.

I glanced around the restaurant. "I think so," I answered.

He took the other setting off the table. Just as he left, I remembered the orange juice.

Andale! Andale! Order up!

I ate and wondered which of the five customers in *Diner* I most resembled. I guess if I had to be one I would be the Texan.

The hash browns and the bacon were very good. The hash browns, the shredded kind I like, were salty, and the bacon was just crispy enough.

"Could you please give to me a Hot Dog and a Root Beer," I mumbled to myself in an Indian accent.

When the waiter reappeared, I caught his attention and reminded him of the orange juice. He was very apologetic and said he wouldn't charge me for it.

"Will there be anything else?"

"No."

"Are you staying with us here?"

I nodded.

"Do you want to put the meal on your room?"

"I'll pay," I said.

As I waited for the bill, I wondered what would happen if I had put the meal on the room and gave him someone else's number. I checked that he hadn't charged me for the orange juice and added the price of it to his tip.

I scanned the restaurant as I walked to the door, checking if Kris was maybe sitting somewhere else. I started to walk to the room to see what happened to her, then changed my mind and went down the stairs and out through the front doors into the driveway. I figured that if I ran into Kris, she would probably want me to accompany her to brunch, and I didn't want to sit for another hour in a dining room. The breeze had grown stronger but it wasn't cold enough for the sweat top so I tied it around my waist. The water of the lake looked choppy. I could see a few powerboats farther out bouncing about. As I walked along the boardwalk toward the town, I imagined it being in the Alps, and I (as someone like Heidegger or Kant) was taking a vacation. During my first year in university I'd taken "An Introduction to Philosophy," and though I hadn't done well in the course I'd enjoyed reading about the lives of the philosophers and imagining myself as one of them, transcending everything, being logical, clear and precise.

"Whereof one cannot speak, thereof one must be silent."
"Snow is white, if and only if snow is white."

These sentences would repeat themselves, and I would feel like I was beyond the people around me.

My reimagining of the town was helped by the chalet-style architecture of the German restaurant I passed.

When I got to the far end of the boardwalk, I turned and started back to the hotel. The beach was beginning to get crowded and I saw one woman sit up and stroke her blond hair back into a ponytail. What would Maria or Sadie think if they came up here? I wondered. For some reason it was easier to think of Maria here than Sadie, maybe because Maria had told me that the town she came from in Mexico was a resort town, and I wondered what it was like compared to this town.

I was halfway through the lobby when I heard Kris. "Trace, there you are."

Her voice sounded a ways off, and it took some time to notice her waving to me from inside the lounge.

She was sitting with a man who I mistook for Michael Daniels. He had the same well-groomed gray hair and rugged but wrinkled face, and his sport jacket looked like something Michael would wear.

"This is my nephew," Kris said introducing us.

"Hi. Richard," the man said rising from the chair, extending his hand.

I told her my name was Richard—Richard!

I tried not to laugh. The handshake seemed practiced, and I had the mental picture of him repeating the gesture over and over again in front of a mirror. He sat back down in the chair. "We were just talking about you."

I nodded politely, then turned to Kris. "You had breakfast yet?"

She raised the Bloody Mary. "Kind of," she said and looking to Richard, laughed.

"Is that an English accent I detect?"

"No," I said.

"It's a speech impediment," Kris said, and drained her glass.

Richard looked uncomfortable. "You've been outside?" he said, resuming his pleasant demeanour. "Is it warm out? It looks windy from here."

"Pull up a chair," Kris said.

"It's not bad," I said to Richard, then to Kris, "I'm going to go swim."

I spent the rest of the day going back and forth from the pool to the games room. At about four o'clock I began to feel nauseous. I went back to my room. Lying on the bed I peered at the digital alarm clock. The air in the room was stale. The digital five turned to a six. I got up and slid open the balcony door and returned to the bed. A breeze came in the room and the drapes billowed in it. The pattern of light changed as the drapes fluttered. I took deep breaths of cold air and tried not to think. The feeling of guilt came over me for fantasizing about Emily and her psychiatrist.

After two or three minutes I was still feeling bad, so I got up and went into the washroom. I turned the cold shower tap on. I put my head right under the shower and the cold water ran down my face and neck and back. My head ached.

When I stepped out, I was shaking. I towelled myself dry and noticed my travel bag on top of the toilet tank. I dug through it and found a box of Gravol. I took out a blister pack. Two pills were left. I popped them out and downed them with a glass of water.

Back on the bed, I started to feel slightly calmer. I don't think it was because of the Gravol—it was too early for it to take affect—rather the expectation that I would feel better made me feel better.

It was freezing in the room when I woke. The door was still open, the drapes flapping in the blue darkness. I stood up, feeling quite drugged. There was a weird sensation in my stomach. I slid the door shut and sat back on the bed. At least the anxiousness was gone.

But I wanted to see people. I picked up the chinos and plaid shirt I'd thrown onto the washroom floor and put them on.

Still freezing, I dug out a sweater vest from my suitcase and stopped in front of a mirror. My hair had a cool dishevelled look, and I imagined myself as some anti-hero in a movie.

Cowboy, you know what you got to do.

Take it easy—I stepped out into the corridor. *You're nineteen years old, you have nothing to worry about. Just a bit high-strung, you've always been that way.*

On the way to the elevator I remembered a night at outdoor school in Grade Seven when I was so frightened of throwing up that I threw up all over this other kid's boots. The next morning Carly, who the boys in my cabin had voted the girl with the best ass when wet, asked if I was alright.

The lobby was different than it had been earlier. The lights had a soft glow to them and the room seemed more sedate than it had been in the afternoon. A man in a tweed sports jacket staggered in the direction of the dining room. I glanced at my wrist and saw I had left my watch in my room. I walked down to the lounge to see if Kris was still there—not expecting that she actually would be. She hadn't come to get me for dinner and I wondered if she'd called, but I hadn't heard.

When I came around the corner, I saw she was seated in the same spot as before. The man called Richard was also in the same chair as before and he sat forward, his elbow on his own knee, his fingers touching Kris's.

He seemed to be in the middle of a story, and just as I got there, he paused and looked up.

"Here's the man himself," he said gaily.

"You're back." Kris looked angry.

"Did you already go for dinner?" I asked.

"Breakfast, dinner, lunch." Kris waved her hand over the glasses on the table. She burst out laughing. Richard grinned politely.

"Have a seat, Casey."

"Trace."

"What was that?" he said and put his hand to his ear.

"Trace," I said. "My name's Trace."

"My apologies." He held out his hand again. I shook it, and pulled up a chair.

Richard glanced from me, to Kris, to me.

"Well, go on," she said, picking up her drink and rattling the ice in it.

He looked like he was struggling to remember what he'd been saying. "So. So when they found her, she'd driven off the dock into the lake."

Kris finished the drink, shaking her head. She set the empty glass on the table and said, "Sad, sad, sad." Then turned to me and said, "Rich was just telling me what a happy place this is!"

Richard looked at me and laughed.

"So…"

"Trace," I said.

"So Trace, what do you do?"

"He's at university right now," Kris said.

"University. In Vancouver?"

"UBC."

"So what are you studying there?"

When I didn't answer fast enough he turned to Kris and said, "Girls?" and laughed.

"I wish," she said, shaking her head.

"I'm just taking general studies."

"He's actually wasting his time." Kris leaned over and took out her pack of Matinée.

"Give the *fucking* young man a break," Richard said. "He's got to find out about life. He's got to live it like I've lived it. I didn't get serious about things until I was at least thirty." He turned to me. "Are you going to go into real estate like your aunt?"

"No."

Kris lit a cigarette.

"Anyway, Trace, what are you drinking? Can I get you something?"

"It's okay," I said.

"Here," he said, rising and reaching into his back pocket. He took out his wallet and took out a twenty. "Get yourself something. Anything. It's on me."

"It's okay."

"Come on! Take it."

"Go ahead," Kris said, gesturing for me to take it.

I went the bar, but I didn't feel like drinking. The thought of alcohol nauseated me. But I didn't want to offend Richard or get in an argument with Kris, so I ordered a Shirley Temple.

"What did you get there?" Richard asked when I got back to the table.

"A Shirley Temple."

He laughed. "That's normally what my eleven-year-old daughter drinks!"

I wasn't very tired. I wanted to talk to someone. Thought about calling Damien or Cameron. Took the phone book from the bedside table in my room and tried to figure the directions for a long distance call. Damien was the first one I tried, but there was no answer. Next, Cam. After five rings, his mother picked up the phone.

There was a drowsy tone to her voice. "Yes, who is it?"

"Hi, Mrs. White. Is Cameron in?"

"*Trace*—do you have any idea what time it is? We're all in bed."

"Sorry."

The line went dead.

I went out on the balcony. It wasn't as breezy as it had been that afternoon. I leaned on the railing. The pools glowed in the darkness. About a dozen people, their voices sounding drunk, stood in the middle of the hot pool, talking. Recalling the sensation of jumping off the ten-metre board at the Aquatic Centre and how it felt to fall a long time before hitting the water, I imagined the feeling of falling toward them.

The sound of the band in the Copper Room came across the grass and it sounded like they were playing "Tie a Yellow Ribbon Round the Old Oak Tree," though I wasn't certain. I looked at the black shape of the mountain against the blue sky and the stars above and wondered if Cam had contacted the Brazilian yet. Could any of what he said be true? Of course the only way to know would be to talk to the girl, which, of course, was what he was not allowed to do.

After a few minutes, my thoughts drifted on to Emily. What had she been trying to tell me?

Leaving the balcony door ajar, I climbed into bed and lay with one sheet covering me and tried to fall asleep. Eventually I reached into my boxer shorts and after considering other scenarios, returned to Emily in the psychiatrist's office.

Kris was at the end of my bed. She was in her kimono housecoat, one leg tucked under her. She was holding a plastic glass of red wine.

"You weren't very nice to Richard."

My vision blurred and I sat up, rubbed my eyes.

"You—NOT NICE to Richard."

I blinked a couple of times before I could see clearly.

"Where is he now?"

"I—DON'T KNOW."

I nodded my head—she was looking at me in a strange way.

"You still haven't done it yet, have you?"

"What?"

"You still haven't done *it*."

"What?"

"You still haven't done it. You're a *virgin*."

"Can you leave."

"What's the matter? Is there something wrong? Are you like Richard?"

She put the glass of wine on the floor and reached for my leg. I pulled it up under myself.

"Leave," I said.

"I'm worried about my 'little nephew,'" she said and laughed.

"Just leave."

"You got a kiss for your Auntie?"

"Leave."

"I'm worried about you."

"*Leave*."

"Don't you want to have some fun? Your *father* liked to have fun."

She crawled toward me. I leaned against the headboard and pulled my foot up in front of me.

"Don't you dare," she hissed.

I stayed in the position.

"Kiss me."

She reached for my ankle and I kicked out at her. I didn't mean to, but I hit her in the face. She fell back onto the floor and I jumped off the bed and ran into the washroom. I closed the door and locked it. I expected her to be right after me.

After what seemed like a long time, her voice came through the door: "Good *niiiight*, Traaace."

A door clicked, and I assumed that she had left. But I wasn't certain. I turned the lights off and slid down onto the floor and listened. The muffled sound of a TV came from somewhere, and someone somewhere flushed a toilet. Under my feet the tiles were cold. As I squatted there, shaking, I drew my legs up and wrapped my arms around and squeezed them. Crouched like that, I rocked gently back and forth and told myself to breathe deeply, to breathe deeply.

After awhile I felt well enough to get up. In the dark I reached around for the sink—I didn't want to turn the light on—and found a washcloth and turned on the right faucet; waited until the water was cold, and soaked the cloth and pressed it to my face, cold water dribbling down my chin and neck.

All things must pass, I told myself, *all things must pass, all things must pass…*

I didn't see Kris until the following afternoon. She was sitting in the outside hot pool, talking to an older woman with very brown and wrinkled skin. I changed direction, trying to duck out of view. But before I could she caught sight of me.

"Oh, here's my nephew," she said.

I made an awkward smile and walked toward them.

"Trace, this is Mrs. Bjornson. She's from North Van, too."

"Hi," I said.

"Her son goes to Handsworth. Maybe you knew him—what was his name again?"

"Andrew Bjornson," said the woman. "But he's quite a bit younger than you. He's in Grade 9."

I shook my head.

"Did you just get up?" Kris asked.

I lied, saying that I did.

"What were we talking about?" she said to the woman.

"Maui. The US/Canadian exchange—"

"Oh that's right," Kris said, becoming animated again. "I have a friend, Michael Daniels—you may have heard of him. He's big in real estate in Vancouver. Anyway, he says there are luxuries and there are needs, and Maui is definitely a need."

The woman laughed.

"He won't stop going to Maui no matter how expensive, and he said—"

When Kris turned to the side I looked at her right cheek behind the sunglasses. It was difficult to see because of the shading from the glasses, but neither the cheek nor the part around the eye appeared bruised. Nor did her forehead.

"Do you realize that I could've bought that same condominium in '73 for fifty thousand. And now it's a million."

"Incredible," the woman said.

"Anyway, I'm getting a bit hot. Trace, do you mind getting my towel. It's on that rock."

As I walked over to grab the towel I wondered if the previous night had happened.

7

3:17 A.M.

"*This is the antichrist*"

"*This is the ANTIchrist?*"

"*Yes.*"

"*THE antichrist?*"

"*Yes.*"

"*Okay…. Well, do you have a name—or does it say Mr. Antichrist on your mailbox?*"

"*You have no idea—No Idea—what you are trifling with.*"

Silence.

More silence.

"*Okay. Tell me—when did you realize you were the Antichrist?*"

"*In grade four.*"

"*You first realized you were the Antichrist in grade four?*"

"*Yes.*"

"*Did the realization come to you all at one moment? Or—*"

"*It began with a series of thoughts.*"

"*What were these 'antichrist' thoughts like?*"

"Let's just say that I knew when things were going to happen. I had prescience."

It wasn't till the third week of classes that I saw Sadie. She was sitting alone at a table in the SUB. Her hair, lighter than it had been in the summer, was almost a platinum blonde. She brushed it back, looked up, and waved me over.

"Trace. You haven't called me."

"I called."

"When?"

"I don't know. Sometime in August. Your mom said you were on Vancouver Island."

Sadie giggled and said, "You don't know?"

'What?"

She laughed. "Here. Sit down." She took the bag off the chair beside her. "Okay, I met this English guy, actually he's Italian—I told you?"

I shook my head.

"Anyway, his name is Antonio. He moved back to England this summer and I wanted to visit him—"

"In England?"

"Yeah," she said laughing. "But I told my parents I was going to visit a friend on Vancouver Island. And they actually believed me. They actually *believed me!*"

She took an envelope of photographs from her handbag and went through them, telling me about her trip. When she came to the ones of her and Antonio together, she said, "These ones, they're just for me," and lay them face down on the table.

I flipped through the remaining photos, the uncensored ones. Most showed Sadie with a young man together and were close-ups. A few had London landmarks in the background. Antonio was thin-boned and had sharp features, quite different from the beefcakes Sadie normally dated.

I was about three quarters through the pile when Hugh and Anna appeared at our table.

Sadie reintroduced me to them and invited them to join us.

Hugh had on the same clothes he always had on, blue jeans, scarf and sports jacket, and Anna wore a blue and white French sailor's top.

Sadie showed Anna the pictures of her trip, and both women giggled when they came to the pictures that Sadie hadn't allowed me to see.

As they did this, I took furtive glances at Hugh and wondered if it really had been him in the Railway Club.

Now, looking at him up close, I wasn't sure.

When they started talking about the oceanography course they were taking, I excused myself and went to the washroom.

At the urinal, there were two posters at eye level.

BE READY FOR TONIGHT

NO MEANS NO

The left one, a condom advertisement, showed a bob-haired girl in a silver cocktail dress dancing in a night club.

Maybe means NO—said the other one—*I don't know means NO. Not now means NO. Later means NO. I have to use the washroom means NO. Not tonight means NO. I have a headache means NO. I'm not sure means NO. Wait means NO. I'm sorry means NO. Stop means NO. I'm sick means NO. Do you have condom means NO. It's not a good time means NO. I'm tired means NO. I don't*

*feel like it means NO. Do we have to means NO… NO…
NO… NO…*

The call came on the last day of September. For the week
before the weather had been clear and warm, but that
morning I'd awoken to find that the rain had returned.
I remember I was lying on the futon in my apartment,
listening to Radiohead's *The Bends* when the phone rang.
Since moving to the apartment I hadn't got many phone
calls, so it kind of startled me.

When I answered I almost said, from force of habit,
"Patterson Realty," but stopped myself. "Hello."

"I'm looking for Trace Patterson. Does he live here?"
said a male voice with an English accent.

"Yeah. That's me," I said, suddenly tense.

"Hello, Trace," the man said, the tone of his voice
familiar but solemn. "I don't know if you remember me.
This is Paul Burgess, Damien's father."

"Oh. Hi, Mr. Burgess." I said, unsure of why he was
calling me, thinking he wanted to ask about Damien's
moods or the things he had said.

But after a long pause, followed by a deep breath, Mr.
Burgess said, "Well, I'm not sure how to tell you this,
but there's been an accident. Damien—he's no longer
with us."

For no more than a second I thought "not with us"
meant "not here but somewhere," that he had gone missing
or had escaped from the hospital. But then I knew.

There was even a longer silence before Mr. Burgess
spoke again. "His mother and I aren't sure what happened
yet, but apparently there was an accident at the hospital—
you knew he was there?"

"Yes."

"Apparently he was in a fight with another patient. They're still investigating the matter and, well, in any case, Damien's funeral is next Tuesday in North Van and his mother and I would like you to attend."

He gave the time and the address and I told him that I would be there.

After I got off the phone I just sat on the sofa for a long time. I don't think I was crying. I was just sitting there.

The phone call, I remember, came in late afternoon and I just remember the room becoming darker and darker.

The days leading up to the funeral something strange occurred. Now that the worst had happened, my fears answered, the jittery feeling that had plagued me for the previous six months died. I would go to bed at eleven and sleep dreamlessly till eight. This contentment sometimes bothered me, but even my guilt or innocence no longer seemed to matter.

The day of Damien's funeral I awoke with a sense of purpose. The funeral was being held at a Catholic church and the night before I'd watched Scorsese's *Mean Streets*, imagining myself as Charlie and Damien as Johnny Boy. I even went so far as to wear one of my father's suits from the late '70s, with flared pant legs and wide lapels. *You look like a pimp*, I told myself, looking at my reflection in the hall mirror.

The weather was clear, and as I drove through the downtown core, it was strange to look at the young women in bright skirts, the men in dark suits striding through the streets, the blue sky between the glass towers and trees still with their leaves—leaves that had been buds when I'd seen Damien in the hospital in the spring—and know that he was no longer a part of it.

In North Van I took the highway to Lonsdale and went up Lonsdale to 24th street. I'd assumed that I could follow the street until I came to the address Damien's father had given me. But after three blocks, East 24th stopped at a dead end in front of a ravine.

I pulled the car to the curb, turned off the engine, and got out. This fat man, I remember, was mowing his lawn, and he stared at me as if he was going to say something, but then went back to mowing.

"No Dumping. Violators will be prosecuted," said the sign in front of the ravine.

I walked up and leaned against the post. Beyond the trees the street began again—I could even see a red Ford parked on it.

I pulled up phlegm from my throat and spat into the ravine. The mower behind me stalled; there was this eerie deadness in the air. I remember feeling then, stronger than I had ever felt before, an intense feeling of futility, that the city was against me. The rain, the canyons, the ocean, the trees, the mountains—all seemed there just to stop me. And I remember getting back into my car with the intention of giving up, going back to my apartment and phoning Mr. Burgess and leaving a message saying that I didn't feel well.

But just before I reached the highway Cocker's version of "With a Little Help from My Friends" started on the radio. Jabbing the off button, I turned east, and took the Lynn Valley off ramp.

After a few more minutes of searching, I found the church. It looked very different from how I'd imagined it. It was one story high and had a flat tar and gravel roof and looked more how I expected a Protestant church to look than a Catholic one. The parking lot was full, so I parked on the street. When I got to the top of the steps, I paused before the large wooden doors, afraid that everyone was going to stare at me when I entered. From inside came the muffled sound of singing. I pulled open the right door.

Four people were standing at the end of the foyer by the entrance to the main part of the church and one of them, an older man with a neat grey moustache, glanced back at me. I'd had doubts about my intentions in coming to the funeral, but the nod he gave reassured me that I was supposed to be there.

Over their heads I could see the altar and the priest. I walked toward the people in the foyer, but then stopped.

The large grey thing—the casket—it was in the middle of the aisle. I moved so that the people standing in front of me blocked my view.

"This past Sunday I celebrated another funeral," the priest said. "It was the funeral of one of our parishioners, Ernie Edwards, Ernie Edwards was eighty-nine. That was a very different funeral."

The words continued and I focused on them. I imagined that this was an evangelist on the TV and that was all it was. I glanced down and quickly looked up—my feet had lined up with the edge of the tile. *Paper slippers. That fag probably wants me dead.*

"—there, there was a feeling of completion, of accomplishment. But here?"

I stared out over the people, wondering if I'd see Cam. I'd left a message on his answering machine, telling him to call me. When he hadn't, I had left a subsequent message telling him that Damien was dead and giving him the time and the location of the funeral.

Near the back was a young woman roughly my age. She wore a black dress and a grey cardigan. She had a large chin but was good-looking, and I wondered who she was and how she was connected with Damien.

"—truly this is a case where it is hard to see God's will."

Was she a cousin? A daughter of his parents' friend? What did these people think about what had happened?

The sermon part over, the service moved to the rituals. I remembered most of the words to the penitential rite.

…sinned through my own fault… what I have done, and what I have failed to do…

I followed the actions of the people around me, kneeling on the hard tile floor and making the sign of the cross, actions I remembered from my two years in Catholic school—they were almost instinctual. Then it was time for prayer.

With my eyes closed, imagining someone was there, I spoke silently inside myself, up toward the darkness inside, and actually felt better.

Afraid, I did it again… and again relief came. A pot had been boiling on the stove and someone had come and taken the lid off, the things ricocheting around in my head found somewhere to go.

I was afraid to wear out this feeling, so after saying "Amen," stopped.

Following the service there was a reception in the gym across the courtyard. I made sure I left the church before they brought out the casket. No one was in the gym when I got there, and afraid that people would come in and see me standing alone, I disappeared into the washroom.

I caught sight of myself in the mirror.

My face contorted, went red, my throat tightened. I seemed to be choking—I watched the face in the mirror and saw that it was doing what it was supposed to be doing, and feeling how it was supposed to be feeling, and I felt something like a painful joy.

I hit the lever of the towel dispenser beside the sink. I cranked down a length of brown paper towel and tore it off. I wiped the tears from my face, but another tear came. It jerked down my check and when it reached my lip, I stuck out my tongue and tasted the hot saltiness.

I was still there, staring at my reflection, when the door swung open behind me.

I ducked into the one toilet stall, and closed and locked the door. I stayed standing. It sounded as if two men had come in. I leaned my head against the wood and pressed my face against the cold, painted surface.

"Very sad, very sad," one said.

The other man grunted. "I can't believe they're not cremating."

"Uh? Oh—I get your meaning."

"Apparently when they stopped her…"

"Terrible," the other man said, and coughed.

That autumn, I saw Sadie only once more. It was the week before Halloween and I was in her area and I couldn't resist the temptation to drop in.

For most of the visit, I just sat on her bed while she took curlers out of her hair and watched *Wheel of Fortune*. At one point I asked her if she still prayed the prayer taped to the side of her night table. She said that she did. I began to explain that I'd begun to pray myself, but before I could explain why she asked me if I thought Vanna White's breasts were real.

Also during that visit, I told Sadie about Cam. I told her everything, except for the part where I accompanied him to the student's homestay house.

"Wow! Is he some kind of stalker?" she asked. She had her back to me and was cutting split ends out of her hair. "You're friends with this guy? He sounds really psycho."

"No. I just know him. He's just an acquaintance."

"My friend, Caroline—you know Caroline, right?"

I shrugged. "Yeah."

"Anyway, there was like this guy—look at this?" She showed me a split end.

Wheel of Fortune had ended before she said, "What was I telling you?"

"Caroline. A guy liked her—"

"Oh yeah. This guy at work. He was obsessed with her. He was so crazy."

"What did he do?"

"I don't know. He just, you know, tried to talk to her and stuff. Anyway, finally she had to get this restraining order. And then the guy, he killed himself!"

Just an acquaintance.

The phrase still haunts me.

The last time I saw him was in the Starbucks on Esplanade. It was sometime in November, about a month after Damien's funeral—the whole summer before seemed like an hallucination.

He didn't say much at first. We sat by one of the windows and he stared out at the rain. Then he asked if I had ever considered visiting a prostitute.

"Not really," I answered.

He nodded, then gazing back outside told me a story about this guy he had met in the police station. The guy visited women who advertized themselves in the back of *The Georgia Straight*. So far this man had visited two. Both were Asian and lived in apartments in East Van. When the guy had visited the first one, she'd stood behind the door until he was completely inside, then closed the door to reveal herself. She was a lot older than she had said on the phone, and her frilly nightgown was see-through, and both he and the woman were embarrassed. She'd tried to suck him hard enough to get the condom on, but finally gave up, saying she was sorry and gave him his money back. The second one—apparently—was better. She had a very lithe body (that was how the guy had described her) and he screwed her for forty minutes.

Cam fell silent.

I was suddenly again conscious of our surroundings.

"...think I'm normally a patient person," laughed the woman across from us. She was holding a baby on her lap. "But this was unreal. I finally had to..."

"Oh yeah!" Cam said. "This guy, he said that the second one could barely speak English, but she pronounced the word 'Fuck' *perfectly*."

"I guess it's an important word for her job," I said, meaning the statement as kind of a joke, but Cam didn't seem to catch it.

"Also," he said, "she ended up giving this guy most of his money back!"

Looking down, I rotated the sleeve on my coffee cup.

"Why are you telling me this?" I finally said.

At first Cam did not seem to hear me. He peered out the window and tapped his fingers on the table. But when he looked back, a conspiratorial grin creased his lips.

Earlier he'd told me that because he'd tried contacting the Brazilian with the letter, the judge had sent him to the hospital, and he now had to report to this officer once a week.

As he told me these things I remember wondering if the two mothers sitting next to us had heard any of the conversation, and what they would have thought if they had. It felt strange to be sitting so close to them, to be living in the same city as them, and yet being so separated.

I also remember that when we left, Cam grabbed a *Georgia Straight* and flipped to the back of it and pointed to an advertisement, saying, "This one looks interesting."

For a long time afterwards, I did not know what to make of that summer. From movies and from the books I read I had come to expect that events could be fit together into some sort of a narrative, that no matter how tangled or twisted the plots or varied the events might be, some theme and direction could be discerned. But here there appeared to be nothing, just random images, remembered sensations, bits of dialogue—it was how it is with an Al Adamson movie, stock footage and outtakes spliced together with only the briefest nod to coherence. (That at least was what I wanted to believe.) But years later, when I began to speak to the people around me about that summer (none of whom I'd known back then) telling them in hurried antidotes and little snapshots about what had happened, finding that one shot *would* lead to another shot, that one scene *would* fade into another scene, that even where the shots did not flow that *that* too was part of the story, I came to see the reason for my reluctance to view "the movie" as a whole, my wilful inability to grasp its significance—for it was only by the seeing it as a whole that my role came into view.

People always say to me when I tell them about Cam or Damien or Alex, "Wow, man, you really cared." But that was not what I saw when I rewound and rewatched those six months in the late '90s (and consider the scenes that did not make this final cut: the scene where I told Cam and Damien to smash Tiff's Porsche, the scene in which I drove Cam to an apartment in East Van, the scene where Alex told me she was going to have an abortion and I remained silent.) What I saw was not someone that cared, what I saw was someone that frightens me.

Acknowledgements

I want to express gratitude to the staff and the students of the UBC Creative Writing Department who helped me out along the way: Susan Juby, Annabel Lyon, Lisa Moore, Annie Zhu, Trevor Corkum, Irina Kovalyova, Jessica Block, Jill Sexsmith, Jessica Michalosky, and Kristin Seeman.

I am particularly indebted to Lee Henderson, without whose initial enthusiasm for my work I may never have continued; Roger Seamon, who has been a indefatigable reader of my work over the years; John Metcalf for his enthusiasm for this novel; Dan Wells for taking a chance on it; and Zsuzsi Gartner, whose belief in me as a writer kept me going, and from whose editing I have learned much.

Finally I would like to thank Miho and our three children, Mina, Curtis, and Rachel for their patience, my grandma for her tireless proofreading and suggestions, my mum for various 'literary' birthday and Christmas gifts (the money for my first Creative Writing class was one of them), and my grandfather for his financial and emotional support.

About the Author

Shawn Curtis Stibbards is a school
teacher who lives in North Vancouver
with his wife and three children. *The
Video Watcher* is his first novel.